The Day Of The White Horse

A Story about Karensa

Jean Cullop

EsteemWorld Publications
United Kingdom

THE DAY OF THE WHITE HORSE

Copyright © 2010 By Jean Cullop

ISBN: 978-1-907011-11-5

First Published 2010 in the United Kingdom, by
EsteemWorld Publications

British Library Cataloguing In Publication Data
A Record of this Publication is available from the British
Library.

For further information or permission, address:
EsteemWorld Publications
United Kingdom.
E-mail: info@esteemworldpublications.com
www.esteemworldpublications.com

By the same author
➤ *Average Alex Brown*

Other books in the Karensa series
➤ *Where Dolphins Race with Rainbows*
➤ *Castle of Shadows*
➤ *Children of the Second Morning*
➤ *Silver Serpent, Golden sword*

Printed in Great Britain for EsteemWorld Publications

Contents

The Lost Kingdom

As far away as yesterday, is an island called Karensa where dolphins race with rainbows and creatures walk freely in the Dark Forest, and broken hearts are healed.

The people of Karensa, who live and speak in the ways of ancient times, were once ruled by a King with perfect love and justice, until one day, everything changed.

Bellum, a Lord of the Palace, disobeyed the King. This brought fear and death to the island. Bellum was forced to leave the Royal Palace forever and people were no longer allowed to approach the King.

Lord Bellum then built a castle from where he planned to one day rule Karensa, Many people followed him and believed the false promises he made.

But this King loved his people more than they would ever know. To save them from death, he sent his own son, Salvis, to die in their place, which broke his heart.
At the moment Salvis died, the captives in Bellum's castle were set free and what had seemed like defeat became victory.

Because he conquered death, Salvis now lives again in the Royal Palace and all who put their trust in him are forgiven and receive the King's power. So it will be on Karensa until the day that Salvis rides out to claim back the Lost Kingdom.

That day draws near.

Chapter 1

A White Horse

Gentle shadows drifted through the Dark Forest, where the branches of snow-clad trees stood stark and bare against the pale moon. Daylight faded into the surrounding mist and once again the island of Karensa prepared to sleep.

Beyond this forest, the Meadow of Flowers led to the castle of Lord Bellum, a peaceful field disguising a destination of despair.

Two horsemen rode across the meadow; both were awesome, majestic figures in the moonlight.

One rider, who came from the castle, wore a crimson cloak that spread against the white snow like blood. His horse was black, as was his hair, as was his heart. Lord Bellum, the King's enemy, who long ago had disobeyed him, was riding out to give battle.

The second rider came from within the Dark Forest. This grey horse was gentle and the rider was dressed in blue, with a gold circlet surrounding his silver hair. Lord Veritan, the King's greatest friend, was riding out to defend his master.

Moving slowly, their magnificent jewels reflected in the snow, these two ancient Lords of the Palace came together at the place where the stream tumbled over stones, and icicles sparkled from the granite rocks.

Bellum's voice was at the same time musical and yet mocking. "So, Veritan, have you come to join me at last?"

Lord Veritan replied steadily, "No, Bellum, I have come to challenge you."

Bellum raised his eyebrows and narrowed his eyes at the same time, a gesture which might have been amusing but instead was menacing.

"Challenge me? How could you ever challenge me? You have no leader. The King is powerless and his son, Salvis, is dead, no matter what superstitious people believe. Stories about him living again in the Royal Palace are nothing more than a vain hope for those who know they are defeated. Dead is dead!"

"Your time is short, Bellum. You are the defeated one. That was decided when Salvis willingly died for the King's people."

Bellum threw back his head and laughed.

"You said it yourself - Salvis died! Oh, Veritan, you are loyal to the wrong people!"

"Salvis lives on," Veritan insisted, "and all those who have put their trust in him will live on too. He will ride out from the Royal Palace on a white horse without blemish and he will destroy every enemy of the King!"

Bellum suddenly stopped laughing. His voice was no longer musical, but filled with venom.

"Veritan, your king is defeated. On the far side of the island, his people live under threat of prison and death should they remain loyal to him. Soon, it will be the same here. Karensa will belong to me and then I shall enjoy the worship that is rightfully mine."

In a single movement, Bellum drew his black sword. Slowly, Veritan slid his own sword from its sheath. The golden blade flashed in the moonlight.

"The golden sword of truth, Bellum," Lord Veritan said softly. "I remind you that my sword can never be defeated. Shall we fight now? Shall we accomplish too soon that which your destiny has decreed?"

Bellum showed no fear, but he sheathed his sword, wheeled around and rode back towards his castle.

Lord Veritan was sad as he thought about how the people were suffering, but as he rode back into the Dark Forest, new hope leapt in his heart.

In his path stood a horse of purest white, with a mane and tail of silver. Its hooves and the tips of its ears were silver too.

Before such perfect beauty, Veritan's own horse bent its front knees and bowed its head to the ground.

"Yes," Veritan breathed. "Oh yes, you are the one!"

The horse whinnied softly then turned back into the Dark Forest, leaving behind silver prints in the snow.

On the other side of the island, a youth pushed open a creaking barn door and stepped warily inside. He knew that nowhere was safe from danger, not even this barn which had once been the meeting place of Jay and the Children of the Second Morning.

It was here that a boy called Esram had told them the story of how the King's son, Salvis, had died so that people could go to the King once more. Salvis now lives forever with the King in the Royal Palace.

Much later, Jay and the others had pledged their lives to Salvis and the King, and they had received the King's special power to help them.

The barn had not changed at all since that day. Jay had never thought he would come here again, but neither had he thought that things here on the far side of the island would be as terrible as they were now.

The warlike government called the Guardians was still in power but they had a new leader, a young man called Hawk; that same Hawk was Jay's older brother.

Hawk was devoted to the Guardians and Hawk showed no mercy. Many of the King's followers had been thrown into prison. Some had even died.

Being Hawk's brother gave Jay no protection for there was very little love between the brothers. Jay had come here to the barn to decide what he should do.

He knew that he could talk secretly and silently to Lord Salvis, and he did this now, asking him for help as though he was there with him in the barn. Jay did not understand how this worked, but it always did. It was something to do with the special power the King had sent to them.

As his thoughts turned towards the Royal Palace, he felt as though he was being wrapped in a warm cloak. He opened his eyes. The barn was bathed in golden light.

"Salvis... is it you?" he whispered. "Are you here? I... I've never seen you, but I know... I know you are here..." and he fell to his knees.

Time stood still as he knelt alone yet not alone. When he got up, he knew what he must do and where he must go. He must leave at once for the High Moor; not even go home to say goodbye.

Even as he left the barn, Jay saw a group of Guardian soldiers riding towards him.

If he was to escape, he must go now and not look back.

The wind was bitter and the low bracken provided small protection. Jay wrapped his cloak around his thin shoulders and pulled the hood over his black hair. Shivering, cheeks red with cold, his small, wiry frame bent double against the wind, he struggled towards the one place that could provide safe shelter.

The High Moor was treacherous to those who did not know the paths that criss-crossed the marshes in which many had sunk to their death.

Jay was not afraid of the High Moor, not even in the snow, for he knew the paths. He was not afraid of the snow. Jay was afraid of other things.

He was afraid of his thoughts.

'That was not Salvis. It was my imagination. I am a coward to run away. Why serve the King? The Guardians look after people better than the King...'

"I belong to Salvis!" he shouted to the wind.

The thoughts stopped. Jay knew they would return.

He struggled to the highest part of the moor, battling against the icy wind that stung his cheeks and tore at his cloak. When at last he turned away from the wind and walked downhill, he was exhausted and thought he could go no further.

Just as he was about to give up and let himself sink into the deep snow, something touched his arm. Arrows of fear prickled his spine until he realised his companion was a horse!

The creature nuzzled him softly. It was a beautiful horse of purest white, the like of which he had never seen. Its breath warmed him and gave him hope. Taking hold of its silver mane, he allowed the white horse to lead him to the safety of a small cottage where he knocked feebly on the door.

It was opened by a tall, sharp featured man with long grey hair and a beard.

Jay stumbled into the cottage but the man caught him and another smaller, rounder man came to help.

"Jay?" The round man gasped. "Carrik, you remember Jay? He is my daughter, Holly's friend."

"Of course I do. Come boy, sit by the fire," the first man cried.

They gave him blankets and a brew of fragrant tea, and when he felt better, Jay was able to relate what was happening in the town. He knew that these two men,

Carrik and Reuben, had no love for the Guardians nor the Guardians for them and for their own safety they were forced to live here in isolation.

They listened intently and with compassion.

Carrik said, "Friend Reuben, there is only one place Jay can go to be really safe."

"I agree, Carrik. He must go where others have gone before him. Jay, you must cross the moor to the other side of Karensa, to a farm where Holly now lives with the family of Morwen and her betrothed, Esram."

"We are sending you to a house that has known much sorrow," Carrik added. "But the people there are loyal and true. You must go to Petroc's farm."

Jay suddenly remembered the white horse and was sorry it had disappeared so soon. Then he realised he would see Esram and Holly again and forgot about the white horse.

Chapter 2

A Jigsaw Puzzle

Rosie had been helping on the cake table since nine o'clock and her feet ached. When someone came to take over, Rosie was pleased to have time to get something to eat and to look at the other stalls.

Every year, Poldawn Church held a fete on the first Saturday in December. It proclaimed the coming of Christmas and raised lots of money for charity.

With the summer visitors gone home and Christmas visitors yet to arrive, hotel staff could relax and today, the whole village seemed to have come to the Christmas Bazaar. It was very busy.

Rosie liked the visitors who came to Cornwall. She enjoyed sharing her home with them, but it was good to keep the village to themselves for a little while.

She had been asked to sing in church on Christmas Eve. Rosie had a pure, strong voice and this year she was writing a special song for Christmas. She had written the first verse but that was all.

A glimpse of Rob Pascoe sent her scurrying under a table in order to avoid him. Rob had asked Rosie to go with him to the school party and Rosie hadn't yet given him a reply because she couldn't make up her mind.

She crawled along beneath the tables and came up on the other side of the room where they were selling toys. Thirteen year old Rosie was too old for toys and started to move away but then she saw that hidden at the back of the table was a jigsaw puzzle; a circular one with a ticket on it saying that it had been checked and no pieces were missing.

As she looked at the picture on the box, Rosie's insides lurched because she recognised the scenes.

Heart pounding, she paid a tall, slim man who she had never seen in the village before.

"You'll find this easy, Rosie," the man told her.

Rosie nodded and moved away. Too late she wondered how a stranger knew her name and too late, she knew the answer. When she turned back to the stall, he had gone.

Pulling a woolly hat over her fair curls, she pushed her way outside, glad of the crisp winter air that stung her cheeks and cooled the tears now streaming from her eyes.

"Salvis?" she whispered. "Salvis don't go. Please come back. I'm sorry I didn't know it was you…"

Her older brother, Luke, found her by the harbour wall, clutching the puzzle to her chest. At once he knew something was wrong.

Some years ago they had been guided by dolphins to a strange island called Karensa which was always surrounded by mist. They returned there sometimes. The adventures they had shared on the island had helped them to understand each other's needs. They had always looked alike, with fair hair and grey eyes, but now they often thought alike too.

"What happened?" he asked. "Why have you bought a jigsaw puzzle? You don't even like them."

Slowly and dramatically, Rosie revealed the picture on the box and watched as his face changed.

"Where did you find this?" he whispered.

"It was with some toys. The man who sold it to me… he… well, he knew my name. Oh, Luke…"

"I thought we'd finished with the island…"

"What shall we do?"

"I don't know. You must have the puzzle for a reason. Maybe we should put it together then see what happens?"

"The man... he said the puzzle was easy. I know who he was... I'm not going back again, Luke! I'm never, ever going back after last time."

Luke said nothing.

They tipped out the pieces of the puzzle onto the table in the dining room because this was the warmest part of their house.

They had never made a circular puzzle before. Where did you start? With a square puzzle they always sorted the straight edged pieces first and made up the frame of the puzzle, then filled in the middle. This puzzle was round so that would not work.

The picture showed several scenes so they took one at a time, starting with a woodland picture because the pieces were easy to find.

"The Dark Forest," Rosie breathed.

Next came the Fisher Village, then a wide bay with dolphins playing in the sea; the Bay of Dolphins. Then Black Rock Bay and the Castle of Shadows and High Moor and...

"Luke, this is Petroc's farm!" cried Rosie. "Even the cherry tree is here."

A tear rolled down her cheek as memories flooded back, sweet memories, but sad.

Soon the puzzle was completed, each picture a place they knew so well. In the centre was a beautiful golden castle; the Royal Palace.

Rosie frowned. "One piece is missing. Look, right in the doorway of the palace. Someone is coming out of the Palace and we don't know who because the piece is missing. Yet the ticket said all the pieces had been counted and they were all there. "

"It must have fallen on the floor then," Luke replied. "Let's have a good look."

They searched everywhere but the missing piece remained missing. Finally, in desperation, Luke decided to move the bookcase to see if it had fallen down the back. Rosie couldn't see how that would happen but sometimes it was easier to agree with Luke than to argue

As they pushed the heavy bookcase away from the wall, some of the books fell on the floor but they were disregarded. Luke was always single minded.

"What's this?" he said suddenly. "Rosie, there is a door behind the bookcase! And look, stairs behind it! I never knew these were here. Come on Rosie."

He placed one foot on the bottom stair but she held back and would not go through the door.

"You know where these will lead, Luke. I told you I'm never going back to the island and I meant it."

"Rosie…" her brother struggled to find the right words. "Rosie, I… maybe we need to go back… I don't know…"

Rosie glared at him. "I so don't need to go back there!"

"Rosie, maybe we should go back. Maybe we've got things to sort out there? I'm going, anyway. Please, Rosie, come with me? Please?"

They stared at each other. Rosie had never known Luke to plead before. He was too proud. He must think this was very important and she had learnt to trust him when making decisions.

Luke took hold of both her hands. Rosie felt a warm, tingling sensation that travelled up her arms. Her knees began to tremble and she knew that Karensa was calling her back to its shores.

"Please, Rosie," he repeated, and this time they climbed the wooden stairs together.

At the top of the stairs was another door and this led to a long, low room which was furnished only with mattresses of straw.

They shivered. The room felt cold after the warmth of their centrally heated house.

They looked through the window and saw a tall, fair youth and a girl with red hair who were working together in a farmyard, clearing away the snow. They were both dressed in the long tunics, loose fitting trousers and boots which all the people of Karensa wore.

"It's Morwen and Esram," Rosie murmured. "Luke, this is Petroc's farm and we are in my old bedroom. But Luke, it feels different now. Why am I so scared?"

"Karensa was always full of danger," he replied.

"Not like this! Never like this! Even Esram keeps looking over his shoulder like he's scared!"

Chapter 3

Holly's Request

Meanwhile, not far from the farm where Luke and Rosie had recently arrived, their old friend Holly had decided that High Hill was made just for snow and just for her.

Deep snow fascinated Holly. She had grown up on the far side of the island where the climate was warmer and snow like this was rare. She loved walking through it, loved the crunching sound it made beneath her boots.

Holly never tired of dragging her sledge to the top of the hill and then hurtling down, landing safely in soft, powdery snow.

The light was beginning to fade but she trudged up the hill for one last time, hauling her wooden sledge behind her. At the top she paused, breathing in the crisp, cold air.

From here she could see most of Karensa. Petroc often came here. Holly wished he was here now, but last year, Petroc had died. He had been the first person to give his life rather than betray the King. He now slept beneath the cherry tree at the farm.

Life had changed at the farm, which was worked now by Petroc's sister, Morwen, and by Esram, who one day she would marry. Everyone still called it Petroc's farm. No-one had the heart to change the name because Petroc had loved it so.

Martha, his mother, still lived at the farm but Uncle Amos had returned to the far side of the island where the Guardians ruled harshly and hated the idea of serving Salvis and the King. Many children had fled across the High Moor to find safety at Petroc's farm.

Holly wished that Morwen and Esram were not always so busy. Holly's other friends, Luke and Rosie had suddenly returned to their own land. They had not even said goodbye. Luke and Holly understood one another because their mothers had both died. Rosie was different because she couldn't even remember her mother.

Holly missed them. She missed Luke. She was lonely. She missed her father, Reuben, who was hiding from the Guardians in a secret place.

It seemed that no sooner had Holly begun to care for someone but they left her on her own. Holly longed for just one friend in whom she could trust.

Standing alone on High Hill, Holly began to speak to Lord Salvis, just in her thoughts. She knew that Salvis would hear her, no matter where she was and take her problems to his father, the King. She didn't understand how Salvis heard her thoughts but she told him about her loneliness.

Nothing happened at all so maybe the King was busy doing King Things? It was growing dark so she prepared wearily for one last ride down the hill, but as she did so, she felt suddenly warm all over. Salvis was never too busy to hear her! He was near.

Just has Jay had done in the barn, she fell to her knees. It seemed the only place to be.

"Is that you, Lord Salvis?"

She had no idea how long she knelt in the snow. She knew Salvis would help her – had already helped, just by being there.

With a light heart she sledged down the hill but this time, when she reached the bottom, she crashed into something solid. The sledge went one way and she went the other.

She scrambled up, shaking snow from her straight, mouse coloured hair. The lovely moment with Salvis had been spoilt. She glared fiercely at the cause of the accident, who was looking quite bewildered.

"Oh, you clumsy boy, why don't you look where you are going?" she stormed.

"Holly?"

She looked closer, then gasped. "Jay! What are you doing here?"

Jay stood up and grinned. "Thank you Holly, for running me down with your sledge and no, thank you for asking, but that great wooden sledge didn't hurt me."

"Oh!" Holly had the grace to blush. Once again she had opened her mouth without thinking. She wasn't really selfish, but sometimes it must seem so to people. "I'm sorry, Jay. I didn't see you. Are you hurt?

"I'll survive."

"What are you doing here?"

"I… I've run away from the Guardians. I walked across High Moor. Holly, you can't imagine what it's like…"

"You are not the first to come," she replied seriously. "Many children have been sent by their parents from the far side of the island to safety," she told him. "You must come home with me, to Petroc's farm. Usually we find a family to take in the children, but you shall stay with us and be part of our family. It will be like when we belonged to the Children of the Second Morning."

Linking arms and leaving the sledge at the bottom of the hill, they made their way towards Petroc's farm.

Jay looked around the kitchen. It was a large room but warm and cosy with a blazing log fire in the hearth and a tempting aroma coming from the cooking pot on the range. Huge cushions were strewn over the floor and a wooden settle stood by the fire. At the other end of the room were a table and benches.

A bed stood close to the fire and on this sat Martha, who owned the farm now that both her husband and son had died. Jay thought that Martha looked old to be Morwen's mother. He was not to know that sickness and sorrow had stolen away her years.

Holly brought him a dish of tea. "Now then Jay," she said bossily, "you have met Morwen and Martha. Esram you already know. Tell us how things are on the far side of the island. I should so love to go home to see my friends… and Father." her voice was sad.

Jay chose his words carefully as he drank his tea.

"Your father is still in hiding with Esram's uncle on High Moor. They are safe and well but they are not free to return to the town… The Guardians have become very cruel!"

"They always were cruel," Holly pointed out.

"With my brother Hawk in charge they are far worse."

"The Guardians once came here," Morwen told him. "The people of the Fisher Village sent them away. They would have no more of them after… after Petroc died… " his voice faded to a whisper.

After a moment or two, Jay continued his story, telling them how Hawk was determined to rid the whole island of the King's followers.

"They said their law was just and fair," Morwen remarked with just a touch of bitterness.

"It is," Jay agreed, "unless you remain loyal to the King. Then you are considered to be an enemy and – what was that noise?"

They held their breath to listen.

"Someone is upstairs," whispered Esram, secretly wishing Amos was still with them.

Morwen tossed back her long, red-gold plait of hair. She peered up the stairs, muttering that all this talk about the Guardians had sent them crazy.

Suddenly she gave a gasp of joy as two figures appears at the top of the stairs; a boy in a grey tunic and brown trousers and a girl dressed in blue whose fair hair was pulled back into a high plait.

"We found our old clothes upstairs," the boy explained, sounding unsure.

The girl added, "We're sorry we left without saying goodbye. That was rude."

Holly squeaked with excitement. "Luke! Rosie!" She did a little dance around the kitchen.

Then, as she realised that King had granted the request she had made on High Hill, she silently thanked him with all her heart.

Her loneliness was over. Three of her friends had arrived at the same time.

How good were Salvis and his father, the King!

Chapter 4

Christmas Carols

"Hark, the herald angels sing..."

Rosie's clear voice echoed through the Dark Forest, the trees and the hush of snow making the notes sound like sleigh bells.

Luke joined in rather tunelessly with *Jingle Bells*, which wasn't really a carol but suited their walk through the snow clad trees sparkling in the crisp Karensa air of the Time of Snows.

The young people had been on the island for almost a week and it was as though they had never been away.

Happy in the safety of their home in Poldawn, Luke and Rosie had never though they would ever return to Karensa yet they were here, and it was as though they had come home.

Soon they were all friends again, especially Holly and Luke who spent time together whenever Holly managed to slip away from her chores.

Morwen was usually helping her mother, who seemed to become frailer each day.

Rosie had been unusually quiet and Luke knew that his sister was hurting inside. To see the cherry tree beneath which Petroc now slept had been painful for both of them, but Luke had accepted that his friend had died and Luke had moved on.

Rosie still held tightly to her pain. Whilst pain was in her heart, Petroc lived in her thoughts. Rosie had a childish love for Petroc and she would not let it go.

Now that Luke and Rosie were alone at last as they walked together to the Feast of Snows in the Fisher Village. They were enjoying being by themselves. They could share things about their life at home in Poldawn.

"I was looking forward to Christmas," said Rosie wistfully.

"We won't miss it," Luke reminded her. "You know time is different here. Christmas will be waiting for us when we get home."

"I know, but…"

"Here we have the Feast of Snows to go to. It's a shame the others couldn't come with us but we'll meet them there later."

"They were busy," she said sadly. It seemed that on Karensa, growing up meant doing more work.

"We shall have Christmas when we –" Luke never finished what he was going to say because right then he floundered in a hidden snow drift.

Scrambling to his feet, he spluttered and brushed snow from his eyes.

"I wish we did have a one horse sleigh, like in the song," he grumbled. "It would be easier than walking. A sledge and dogs would do. Actually, that would be fun."

Rosie laughed at him. "You're out of practice. On Karensa, we walk. I like walking through the snow here. It's not slushy like at home. Here it stays around for ages and it's crunchy."

She was laughing, but somehow her eyes didn't match her mouth. Her eyes didn't laugh.

Luke was feeling more than a little guilty that he had persuaded her to return to the island. She was finding it hard to come to terms with Petroc not being here any more.

"Rosie, are you sorry we came back? Maybe I was wrong…"

"No, not sorry… well yes, in a way I am." Her voice was no more than a faint whisper. "It hurts, Luke. I thought the hurt had gone but it hasn't. Morwen and Esram are going to be married and that's lovely but Karensa without Petroc is not the same."

"It can't ever be the same again. You have to let Salvis help you get over it."

Rosie was not used to a brother who cared so much. As though he read her thoughts, he added,

"I promised Petroc before he died that I would look after you. That last time…"

"Did he ask you to do that?" she said wonderingly.

Luke nodded. "He did… but… I'd be here for you anyway. We've shared a lot together, Rosie."

"More than most brothers and sisters," she agreed. "But… I do know Salvis will help me, only… not yet. I'm not ready yet…" She made a determined effort to brighten up. "Let's sing another song. I was writing one for church, for Christmas. I've written a verse but not the chorus. Do you want to hear it?"

She began to sing,

> *"Sweet baby asleep in a manger of hay*
> *In a stable so cold and far away,*
> *We know that you live in our hearts today,*
> *We worship you now, at Christmas."*

Rose had a beautiful voice. The notes were carried deep into the Dark Forest and woodland creatures stirred from sleep to listen.

"Do you like that song?" Rosie asked nervously.

"Well," Luke hesitated. "I do like it, Rosie, but the words are a bit… well… young for you and me. What is the tune? I never heard it before. Did somebody in the music group find it?"

Rosie blushed. "No they did not! I wrote it myself! You sing it to the beat of a drum, like a heart beat."

"That's wicked cool! You really do have a gift, Rosie. You should use it more."

Praise indeed from someone who did not readily give praise.

"I s'pose so... but... maybe it's not for here? After all, they don't have Christmas here."

Luke thought about this. "Well, in a way it was because of Christmas we came here, because you found the jigsaw at the Christmas Fete. Rosie, I think you wrote the song for Karensa."

"But I didn't know I was coming here!"

This awesome truth made them stop and think and for a little while they stood in silence. As they waited, there was movement in the thicket.

Coming towards them was a horse of incredible beauty, pure white, with a silver mane and tail.

"It's a white horse!" Rosie whispered needlessly.

The horse stopped in front of them and Luke put out a hand to stroke it, but even as he moved, the creature whinnied, tossed its head and disappeared again into the Dark Forest, leaving silver prints in the snow.

"Only Lord Salvis may lay hands on the white horse," said a deep voice behind them and they were startled to see Veritan, Lord of the Palace, looking down at them from his large, grey horse.

The Lord of the Palace inclined his head in greeting. "Luke, Rosie, it is well that you are here on Karensa. Luke, you were there when Lord Bellum first disobeyed the King and was sent away from the Royal Palace. It is right you are here now because soon, all things will be made new. Time is short."

Lord Veritan looked exactly as they remembered. If everything else changed on Karensa, Veritan would remain the same. He still wore a gold circlet over his long, silver hair. He was still dressed in blue, the colour of truth and he still carried his golden sword of truth at his side. His name meant Truth. He would always be true to his King.

Luke and Rosie bowed in the way they had been taught. They must kneel only to the King or to Salvis, his son, but it was respectful to bow their heads to a Lord of the Palace.

"You may not touch the white horse," Veritan repeated. "He is reserved for Lord Salvis alone."

"What is he reserved for?" Rosie asked.

"It will not be long now until the day Lord Salvis needs him. Look to the Day of the White Horse. Before it dawns, many troubles will beset the King's people."

"There have been troubles already," Luke replied.

"And there will be many more. Fear will increase. So will lawlessness, as men's love grows cold. Look to that day, both of you. When skies grow dark remember that very soon, Salvis will return. And Rosie, you have a very special voice, but be careful of what you sing and where you sing it. Others may have heard you today."

With those chilling words, he turned his horse and rode away, leaving them alone, and disturbed.

Only they were not alone because someone really had heard Rosie's song. Unseen by the young people, Lord Bellum had been drawn towards notes of such purity.

Bellum loved music. Before he had been sent away from the Royal palace, he had often sung for the King.

Rosie was singing again, but this time it was another song. Her voice rekindled memories for Bellum, memories of the days when he had made music for the

King. *If only the King had been willing for Bellum to accept the worship that his music stirred in men's hearts!* He had forced Bellum to disobey him.

But the King's word insisted that men should worship the King and none other. He was the One King whose worship he could not share because his was the greatest love and justice ever, far beyond the understanding of his people.

Bellum saw and Bellum heard and Bellum was determined that one day, this maiden would lift her voice to praise Bellum, not the King.

Chapter 5

When Love Grows Cold

The village square was warmed by braziers for people to celebrate the Feast of Snows, but in spite of their heat, Jay was shivering. It was much colder here than at home. Even the thick, woollen cloak Esram had loaned him did little to keep him warm.

He thought about the farmhouse he had left behind on the far side of the island. There would be a fire blazing in every room and comfortable chairs and linen sheets on the beds.

In this place he didn't even have a bed! He slept on a straw mattress on the floor.

Holly saw that he was shivering and felt sorry for him.

"You will get used to the cold, Jay. At least here we are safe. We can serve the King without being afraid." He did not reply, so she added, "Let's catch up with Esram and Morwen."

It seemed as though everyone from the village and the farms was here today, putting aside their work to crush into the village square for this annual celebration.

Holly had the ability to somehow get where she wanted to be, so despite the crowd, they soon found their friends

Morwen was showing off a new bracelet made from strips of coloured leather, woven together.

"Look what Esram has bought," she said happily. "He has one for himself, too. They will remind everyone that I belong to him and he belongs to me."

Then she decided that Holly deserved a gift too because she had worked hard on the farm and asked for nothing in return except food and shelter.

"Holly," she said. "See how well these ribbons would look in your hair." She held up a length of gold satin.

"As well as anything could look on me," Holly sighed. She had a plain face and straight, brown hair. She would love to be pretty like Morwen or Rosie, but she had realised a long time ago that people liked her for who she was, not what she looked like. It didn't stop her wishing, though …

Esram bought the ribbons and Morwen promised to put them in Holly's hair when they got home. They were all hungry so Esram went in search of something to eat, just as Luke and Rosie arrived.

They had agreed with each other that they should not mention the white horse until they were certain they would not be overheard.

Rosie found keeping secrets hard. To focus her mind on other things, she grabbed Holly's arm and dragged her off to watch the entertainment.

Morwen had avoided being alone with Luke since he and Rosie had returned to Karensa. They had once been close friends, but now that Morwen and Esram were betrothed things were different. Young people grew up quickly on the island.

"You have grown strong," she observed, placing her hand on Luke's arm. Luke played rugby and was sturdy and muscular.

Morwen was nearly as tall as he. Her green eyes and his grey eyes were level. Morwen shivered. There was something about Luke that almost scared her. He was hasty and hot tempered in a way she could never understand.

"And you have grown fair," he replied, speaking in the island way which was now second nature to him.

"Oh, I know you are promised to Esram," he added hastily. "That's how it must be, but it doesn't stop me caring about you and I know you care about me."

"We shared many dangers," she said slowly. "The dangers brought us close, that is all."

Luke was saved from answering by Esram himself, carrying hot pies. He did not ask why Morwen looked disturbed. He trusted her. Like Veritan, her word was true and she would never let him down.

Somehow, Rosie had sensed that food was on offer and pushed her way back again, with Holly hanging for dear life on her arm. Rosie was not as skilful at getting through the crowd, but she was very good at finding food when she was hungry.

Rosie loved food. It annoyed her friends because she never put on weight, no matter how much she ate. Even Morwen, who was the most charitable person, had once remarked that Rosie's huge appetite and slim waist were simply not fair.

The pies warmed them and satisfied their hunger and soon everyone was ready to explore the Feast of Snows.

In the days before Lord Bellum had rebelled against the King, the Feast of Snows was held in the courtyard of the Royal Palace. Now the Palace gates were closed and so the Feast was held here, in the village square.

Since the government called the Guardians had been sent back to the far side of the island, things had gone well for the people of the Fisher Village and its surrounding farms. Fish had been plentiful and the soil obediently yielded fine crops and provided rich pasture for the farm animals.

If one family was in need, another family with plenty would always help them.

So why was there unspoken fear?

This new prosperity meant that most people were free to enjoy the holiday and there was much to see. There were acrobats, jugglers, fire-eaters, musicians and even dancing. Food was plentiful and the scent of roasted chestnuts and hot pies permeated the village.

Rosie compared the Feast of Snows to the bazaar in Poldawn, and she remembered the jigsaw puzzle.

After an enjoyable afternoon, she was suddenly hungry again. Skilfully, she steered her friends towards another pie stall. The owner of this stall was a plump, fair-haired woman who seemed pleased to see Rosie.

"Do you not remember me, child? You should! Once, you stole from me!"

Rosie frowned, but then she beamed widely. "You are Mara! I do remember. You were so kind to us and I'm sorry I stole your pies but we were very hungry."

"I know," Mara replied. "To show there are no hard feelings I shall give you an apple tart – hey – what are you boys doing? Leave my stall alone!"

Three youths were apparently intent on spoiling her supplies, laughing as they pressed their fingers through the cakes and pies so that no-one could buy them.

When Mara shouted at them, they threw the entire stock to the ground, and then pushed away through the crowd, all the while laughing loudly.

Luke, who was the nearest, tried to stop them and Esram and Jay were not far behind, but to their astonishment, the crowd turned on them

"Do not interfere in what is not your business," one man growled roughly.

"But they did wrong," cried Rosie. "They have ruined Mara's supplies! How can she sell them now?"

"What is that to you?" asked a woman who was holding a baby, jigging it up and down.

"Mind you own affairs!"

"Who told you to come to the Feast of Snows? It is for island folk, not strangers!"

"They are hardly strangers," Mara pointed out. "Good folk they are, to help me."

"You would do well not to accept their help," another woman advised. "And the size of you, Mara, you would do well to go without food for a while!"

Others laughed as Mara scrabbled on the ground trying to rescue what remained of her pies.

Rosie held her breath and said nothing. Once again she experienced the fear she had sensed the moment they had returned to Karensa. Why had the people become so uncaring and rude?

Even as the thought crossed her mind, she recalled Lord Veritan's words, 'lawlessness will increase… men's hearts will grow cold…think on the white horse…'

"They are not really strangers," said Esram, trying to keep the peace and knowing that the island people respected him for the way he had taken over the work on Petroc's farm.

"They do not belong here and that makes them strangers. You also, boy, you with the black hair, you do not belong here either!"

"I was born on Karensa!" Jay protested. "You cannot say I do not belong?"

"We can! Get home and stay with your own kind!"

With one accord, they descended on the group of young people, shaking their fists and throwing clods of frozen earth, forcing them back across the square.

The young people were scared and when they reached the outskirts of the village they broke into a run, but the villagers gave chase.

Esram led them into the Dark Forest and safety, but Rosie, who was running a little behind the others, caught her foot and sprawled full length in the snow.

She lay stunned and helpless as the crowd drew nearer, their curses louder and more menacing.

Trembling, she struggled to her knees. She reached for something to hold to and a hand lifted her up.

"Come, maiden, the hounds have forsaken their quarry," said a deep voice. "They all went home."

Rosie hoped against all hope, knowing that on Karensa, Lord Salvis sometimes left the Royal Palace.

It was not Salvis. He looked a little bit like Salvis - tall and slim with light brown hair - but his eyes were pale where Salvis had dark eyes.

"Who are you?" she whispered.

"My name is Rolf. Are you hurt?"

"No... just out of breath. How did you make the people go away?"

The man smiled. "I am a friend sent to help you."

Rosie was puzzled. Did he mean that Salvis or Veritan had sent him? Rolf reminded her of someone and the thought niggled at her. She couldn't think who he reminded her of, but it was someone she knew well.

"Who are you?" she asked again.

Rolf smiled in return but his eyes did not light up with the smile. When Salvis smiled, it seemed as thought the whole of Karensa smiled with him. This man smiled with his lips but not his eyes.

Chapter 6

A New Government

Luke had been dreaming. He could only half remember the dream. He knew that it was about Poldawn.

Cold morning light filtered through the window shutters; farmers got up very early. Rain lashed the shutters. It would wash away the last of the snow but it was still bitterly cold in the draughty attic where the boys slept.

They had been on Karensa for several weeks and the Time of Snows was moving towards the Time of New Birth, but Luke still missed the comforts of home, especially central heating. Maybe he could introduce central heating to Karensa? He would make loads of money and live in a big castle like Bellum or the King.

The thought made him smile, but the truth was that the island would never be his real home.

Esram and Jay were still asleep so Luke could sneak a few extra minutes in his warm bed and in the pleasant, comfortable state of being not quite awake, the dream returned.

He was on the beach in Poldawn. It was summer and he and his friend Rachel were paddling in the surf. Rachel turned to look at him and suddenly she became Morwen. Rachel had gone.

He woke up. Esram and Jay were shouting at him to get out of bed.

After breakfast, Martha asked for two volunteers to go to the village for supplies.

"We need bacon, we need honey and we need flour. Our stocks are running low," she said. "The visiting children have used our reserves."

"Oh, I do not complain!" she added hastily, seeing that Luke, Rosie and Jay looked dismayed. "It is the work the King gave us to do, to shelter the children from the far side of the island and find them homes. The King will meet our needs to do this."

Rosie's lip quivered. "What about us, Martha?" she asked in a wobbly voice.

Martha made a clicking sound through her teeth. "Child, you know you and Luke are part of our family. But there have been many, many children before you came."

"It's like having two homes," said Luke, thinking again about central heating.

Rosie said nothing at all.

The task of fetching the supplies went to Rosie and Jay.

No-one had been to the Fisher Village since the Feast of Snows, so they were apprehensive that the villagers might chase them away again.

But supplies had to be bought. Sometimes you must set aside your fear and simply trust the King.

Rosie was especially concerned. If it had not been for that man called Rolf, what would have happened to her that day? Rolf had left quickly so the others had not seen him and Rosie wondered if she had seen him at all.

As for the white horse, only she and Luke had attached any importance to it. What they had thought was exciting news fell flat when they related their story.

As Rosie and Jay walked deeper into the Dark Forest, a watery sun filtered through the trees.

"I had not seen you for ages, Rosie," said Jay. "The last time we met was when we all rescued Esram and Carrik from the Guardians."

Luke and Rosie had once stayed on the far side of the island. They had not liked living there, but had made some wonderful friends, like Holly and Esram and Jay.

"You are not safe then, in your town?" Rosie asked. "But surely your brother is the leader of the Guardians?"

Jay gave a short laugh that was not really a laugh at all.

"Hawk and me, we don't get on," he replied. "We never have. We hate each other."

Rosie didn't know what to say. Luke had once been quick tempered and angry because Dad married again and he thought Rosie and Dad would forget their real mother. They didn't hate each other though. They quarrelled, but the quarrels never lasted long.

Jay scuffed the grass. "Hawk never got on with our parents. He says I'm the favourite. I feel a bit sorry for him because he never seems to please Mother and Father and he really is clever and brave."

"You're brave too," Rosie replied. "You used to be our leader. I believe you would fight the Guardians on your own if you had to!"

"I'm not brave. I always wanted to be like Hawk!"

After walking in silence for a while, Rosie confided in Jay that she still missed Petroc.

"I never met him," said Jay. "We heard that a boy had been killed by the Guardians and we were shocked. I didn't know he was your friend."

"He was more than that, Jay. I believe that when we grew up we would have been promised, like Morwen and Esram. Luke says I should ask Lord Salvis to take my sadness away, so we can go home."

"Do you miss your home?" Jay was thinking about his own home and his parents.

"Yes, I do this time. I never really wanted to come back to Karensa. It would be better if there were other people here from our world instead of me and Luke being the only ones."

Jay's answer left Rosie speechless.

"You're not the only ones. Oh, you probably are right now, but years ago there were others. My mother told me about them." He smiled a secret smile as island people often did when talking about their home. "Karensa is very special to you and Luke, Rosie but it has been special to other people too. My mother once said that those who are hurting come here to be healed. You are not the first."

The incident with Mara seemed to have been forgotten by the people in the Fisher Village. They were not friendly, but they served the children politely.

After they had finished shopping, Rosie suggested they went down to the harbour where they could watch the boats coming and going.

Rosie pointed out some landmarks to him as they sat on a stone wall in the sun.

"Down that path is a sandy cove where we used to swim. There is a path leading from the farm, but it is not often used. It goes along the cliff and Martha says it's not safe." She pointed in the other direction. "Over there is the headland where Petroc used to fish and beyond that … beyond that is the beach where Luke and me first arrived when the dolphins brought us here… oh, it's so long ago!"

"Maybe you should go home from there, then." said a voice behind them,

Rosie jumped and nearly fell into the water, but it was only a group of young children who were repeating what they had heard adults say.

"Go back where you belong!" shouted another child.

"We do not want you here!" yelled a little girl of perhaps six or seven.

Sometimes at school, Rosie was laughed at because she went to church and she had found that the best way of dealing with this was to be friendly.

"Are you here all on your own? Where are your – oh, you've hurt your hand, little girl! How did you do that?"

The children were taken by surprise.

"She fell over," said one of the boys grudgingly.

"Well, she needs to go home so that her mother can wash and bandage it," said Rosie. "That's to stop you getting an infection."

The little girl nodded although the idea of infection would be unknown on Karensa.

Unexpectedly, the biggest boy asked, "Do you belong to the King?"

"Don't you?" asked Jay carefully.

"Not any more. What is the King like?"

"Very kind," said Rosie thoughtfully and she would have said more but the children ran away.

Jay and Rosie stared after them. The children's behaviour had unsettled them.

The loud knock on the door at supper time was unexpected. Esram answered it warily, but it was only their old friend, a man called Raldi who was a carpenter and had helped them many times in the past.

Raldi explained, "I had to tell you the news before you heard it from another and thought me rude."

Martha invited Raldi to stay for supper but he refused and looked embarrassed.

"Thank you kindly, but I shall not stay. I have come to tell you that this day there has been a meeting and a certain decision was made."

"What is that decision?" Martha asked quietly, sensing that all was not as it should be.

"My friends, now that the Guardians have gone away, folk need a government, to make laws and uphold peace."

"Why do we need a government when we have the King?" Esram wanted to know.

"Where is the King? He never leaves the Royal Palace. I have been asked to lead a council to do this work," Raldi replied.

"Raldi, you are our dear friend." Martha told him. "It seems we must accept this council but I believe that a mistake has been made and this decision will not be good for Karensa. I believe we are better to listen only to the King."

"Your words are noted, Martha," said Raldi in a cold voice. "I came tonight out of respect for this family. I bid you good-bye"

Supper was eaten in silence and later, when they sang their evening praises, they were subdued and there was no sense of the King being with them at all.

This had never happened before and they went to bed that night with a sense of deep foreboding.

Chapter 7

Rolf

"I like the Time of New Birth."

Holly breathed deeply of the scent of the bluebells that she was carrying.

"Me too," Rosie agreed. "The Time of Snows is so hard, then all at once it's warm and flowers are everywhere."

Holly, Rosie, Luke and Jay had been for a walk and Holly could never resist gathering flowers.

Rosie believed that flowers should be left to grow wild but Rosie's Cornwall was not like the island of Karensa, where flowers grew more abundantly.

The Dark Forest, once shrouded in silent snow, now resounded with birdsong.

Such a day made you feel like singing and Rosie began to sing her special Christmas song."

"Is that Lord Salvis in the song?" Holly asked.

"No, not really," Rosie stammered.

"It's about our world," said Luke, to get her out of trouble, then quickly led them on to talk about something else.

"Has anyone else seen that white horse?"

"Maybe you imagined it," Holly replied unwisely.

"We both saw it!" Rosie cried. "We saw it, Holly. We really, actually, saw the white horse."

"There must be lots of white horses," Jay pointed out.

"Not like this one," Rosie insisted in hushed tones. "Oh, this horse was so special! I can't explain it. When you see it for yourselves, you'll understand. Like when you see Rolf you'll believe he exists and I didn't just imagine him."

"That will not be long then," said a deep voice coming from the direction of the Royal Palace.

They span round to see a tall, slim man walking behind them. Rosie laughed and clapped her hands.

"Rolf! I've looked everywhere for you!"

"Now you have found me," the man smiled.

The others were staring rather rudely. At first Holly had thought this must be Salvis as he appeared to have come from the Royal Palace.

Luke had thought that too, and his heart missed a beat, but this was not Lord Salvis. This man's eyes were the wrong colour; they were pale. Salvis had eyes as dark as night and as gentle as a father's love for his child. This man's eyes were smiling, but cold.

"Sit here with me," Rolf invited them. "Tell me about yourselves. Rosie, teach me your song." He sat down on a fallen log.

It seemed natural to obey him. There was something about this man that drew people to himself. If he was not Salvis, they decided, he must know Salvis very well. Perhaps he was a friend?

For a long time they sat with him and talked and Rolf told them deep secrets about Karensa, just like Salvis used to do when they all lived in a cave in the Bay of Dolphins.* The young people found they could talk to Rolf as they had once confided in Salvis.

Then without warning, Rolf stood up and said he must go and he left them as quickly as he came.

And with his departure, Lord Veritan arrived.

---

*　*Where Dolphins Race with Rainbows*

Jay's mouth fell open. He had never seen Veritan before. Rosie whispered that this splendid giant was a Lord of the Palace and very special.

As always, Veritan wasted no time in saying what he had come to say.

"My children, I am here for a purpose. I am the King's messenger and I have come with a warning from the King that you must be vigilant."

Fear flickered in Luke's heart. For Veritan to leave the Royal Palace meant this must be important. Surely Veritan was not talking about Rolf?

"Lord Veritan… this man… Rolf…"

For a brief moment, Veritan's splendour faded, but just as quickly returned. It reminded Luke of at home, when the weather was bad and the lights dimmed and then came back to full power again.

"Be vigilant, children," repeated the Lord of the Palace and then he rode away.

Days passed and life turned as always on the farm. Soon, the Time of New Birth became the Time of Plenty and with that, a new contentment came to the Fisher Village and the surrounding farms. The new council led by Raldi brought in laws which were fair to everyone and life was easier than ever before.

Despite this, some of the younger people began to rebel against the new rules, saying they robbed them of their freedom.

After dark, when good people were asleep, these young men would run wildly through the village, shouting and throwing stones.

Raldi's new council decreed that to avoid these riots, every person must be in their own home by sunset.

The younger people were furious at this restriction and it was not long before news of rebellion reached Petroc's farm. Some young men had invaded the village, smashing down fences and damaging homes.

A command was issued that each household must help repair the damage. Luke and Esram went along to represent Petroc's farm.

The boys were given the task of repairing fences and they worked side by side, enjoying each other's company.

Luke and Petroc had almost been like brothers and after he had died, it had been Esram to whom Luke had turned for friendship.

"Morwen grows fair," Luke remarked, speaking easily in the way of the island people.

Esram did not look up. "She was always fair," he grunted by way of a reply.

"Did she... did she ever speak of me... us... when we were away?"

Esram stared at his work and spoke as though talking to himself. His voice was distant – almost sad.

"At times, when the air was still, or when we sat with Martha by the fire, each one thinking our own thoughts, then Morwen would speak of you and Rosie. None of us could ever forget you."

Luke felt a rush of friendship for this tall, fair haired youth who had little to say but offered unconditional friendship.

"Esram ... Petroc and me, we once pledged we would be brothers. Could you... could we..."

"No Luke," Esram said gravely, at last putting aside his work. "Your friendship with Petroc was special. I cannot take his place and would not want to. You and I shall always be friends. Petroc would want it that way."

They were silent for a moment because Petroc had been special to them all. The mention of his name caused them to think kindly about the red haired youth who had died so bravely for his King.

Luke gave one deep, sad sigh that spoke volumes and this broke the silence.

"If we are to finish this fence before supper, we had better get on with it. Look, even Rolf is helping out. He's mending a roof over there."

Esram frowned. "So that is the famous Rolf? He reminds me of Lord Salvis, to look at."

"I know. We all thought that at first, but he's not like Salvis at all really, so why does he look familiar?"

Their voices carried and Rolf must have heard them because he climbed down from the roof he was mending and hurried away.

Chapter 8

The Battle Continues

While Luke and Esram were occupied mending fences in the village and Jay was busy splitting logs, Holly went to High Hill on her own, leaving Morwen and Rosie to cook the family meal.

In a chair by the kitchen range, Martha slept peacefully. Morwen had slipped a cushion beneath her head and covered her with a blanket, for even though it was now the Time of Plenty, Martha was often cold.

Rosie felt a twinge of regret for days long ago when Martha was plump and cheerful and energetic. She had looked after Luke and Rosie as if they were her own.

These must have been Morwen's thoughts too.

"Ever since Lord Bellum disobeyed the King, people have grown old very quickly," she said, pushing a strand of hair out of her eyes. "Life used to be free from pain but now there is sickness and death. Some mornings, Mother finds it hard to get up because her joints are so painful. Are things the same in your world, Rosie?"

"Well … people are sometimes ill, even babies and children. My own mother died when I was very small. Luke can remember her, but I can't."

Morwen was contrite. "Rosie, I forgot that. I am so sorry. How could I be so unthinking? How could I?"

"It doesn't matter. I forget about it myself most of the time. Stacey is like a mother now. My real mother is just a photo in a frame."

Morwen frowned. "Photo?"

"A picture then. A likeness."

Morwen still didn't understand because there were no such things as pictures on Karensa.

Flour had been spilt on the table and Rosie drew a face in it with her finger. "Like that, only much better."

"I see … and that shows you what your mother looked like?" Morwen sounded doubtful.

Rosie quickly erased the drawing. Right now, she wanted very much to go home. She wanted chips for tea and she wanted to watch TV instead of going to the praise meeting. She wanted her favourite magazine to read. She wanted a proper bed, not a straw mattress.

She missed her dad and Stacey and Pepper the dog. She wanted to run her fingers through Pepper's silky fur.

But she also wanted to be near Salvis. She wanted to be in the place where Petroc had lived.

Impulsively she gave Morwen a hug and in so doing, covered the older girl's tunic with flour. Morwen tried to wipe it off but a mark was left on the soft, cream wool.

"No matter," said Morwen, trying gallantly not to show that she was upset. This was the first time she had worn the tunic. Once it had been washed, the colour could fade and she suited the rich, dark cream. It matched her red-gold hair and green eyes.

"Look at Jay," she said to change the subject. "He has almost finished splitting those logs. He must have worked some fast!"

"Do you like Jay?"

Morwen laughed. "Of course I do. Why?"

"I don't know. Jay and Holly were friends long before I knew them. They got on well together."

"And you need a friend too," said Morwen wisely. "You miss Petroc."

Rosie nodded miserably, not trusting herself to speak.

"There are no other people here who are from my world, Morwen. Jay told me others had been here from our world. Did you ever hear of others?"

Morwen shook her head. Her heavy plait swung from side to side. "My father always said that those who were hurting came to Karensa to be healed. I never knew any, though, only you and Luke. It must have been a long time ago -"

Jay crashed into the kitchen.

"Folk are coming to the farm and they don't look friendly!" he shouted. Jay did shout when he became excited.

Even as he spoke, a family of fisher people came and stood at the door; father, mother, a youth and two younger children. They did not look friendly. The man had picked up the axe which Jay had left outside.

Morwen kept a cool head, aware that if these people meant them harm, there was little they could do to stop them.

She whispered to Jay and Rosie to leave the talking to her and sent a silent plea to the King to help them from the Royal Palace. She hoped Martha would stay asleep.

"How can we help you, good people?" she asked in a calm voice, hiding her inner turmoil.

The man spoke up. "We would see your mother."

"My mother is asleep. I am Morwen. I can speak for my mother."

A sneer crossed the man's face. He had expected to speak to the head of the household.

"If you say so, *Mistress Morwen*," he said, scornfully stressing her name.

The woman did not want an argument. "The reason we have come here today is that our family has no food. My husband's nets are damaged and he has lost good fishing time," she explained.

Morwen stared blankly.

"We know that the farmers have plenty," the man continued. "We have come for a donation from your store as is the custom."

Tiny prickles of fear crept across Morwen's scalp. They travelled down her neck and her spine. Struggling to keep her voice steady, she refused to allow either Jay or Rosie to help her. The responsibility was hers.

"Sir, we are not as wealthy as you suppose. We do have a store but it is only enough for our own household. If you are in need you should go to Raldi and the council."

The woman spoke up. "This we have done, maiden, and they have sent us here."

"Raldi... Raldi sent you here?" Morwen's composure started to crumble. She could not believe they had been so badly used by their oldest friend.

"He said you have a store of grain and should give some away," the family insisted, all at the same time.

Jay, Rosie and Morwen were unsure of what to do but at that moment, Martha awoke and struggled to the door, her face still flushed from sleep. When Morwen explained what was happening, Martha calmly asked Jay to fetch a sack of grain and some salt meat from the store.

The family seemed satisfied with this and clutching the food, they went away, saying they meant the farm no harm, but must have food.

Once they were safely out of earshot, Martha said they must find somewhere safe to hide their food store.

"Keep a little on view, for if we hide it all, people will be suspicious. Daughter, we must be ready. You may be sure this is not the last time people are sent here for food. We cannot give to everyone who asks, for we would ourselves starve. The King's followers are not liked any more. The people have gone after the new way of this council. Will they never learn that the King's way is the only way that works?"

But... Raldi..." Morwen exclaimed. "After the last time when the Guardians were here with their silver serpents... after Petroc died... I cannot believe this of Raldi!" *

Her mother smiled wryly. "Since he became leader of this council, Raldi no longer comes to our praise meetings. He does not wish it to be known that he is a follower of the King. Children, this is not the first time we have been on our own. We survived before and we shall survive again, but oh, I did not think to see those terrible times return and oh, what a price we paid!"

Rosie quietly slipped her hand through Martha's arm.

"The battle isn't over, Martha. It is the same in our world. The struggle will go on until Salvis returns."

That night, when they came together to praise The King, Rosie sang her song for them. She had written a chorus.

"Innocent one, gentle and meek,
Friend of the poor, friend of the weak,
Live in my heart today."

She sang it again, this time using the secret words the King had given them when he sent his special power; words older than time and sweeter than tomorrow's dawn. **

Others joined her in a wonderful chorus of praise.

Then Morwen stood up and there was silence because they all knew she had a special gift of hearing what the King wanted to say to them.

---

*   *Silver Serpent, Golden Sword*
**   *Castle of Shadows*

"He's coming soon!" she exclaimed. "Salvis is going to return and he will ride from the Royal Palace on a white horse and Bellum will be defeated forever. Then, Karensa shall be as it was meant to be!"

Everyone cheered and clapped and then they sang again in those special words. The message from the King gave them hope.

Praise sprang from deep within their hearts, in the place which belonged to the King alone.

Troubles would come their way, for Lord Veritan had said this would be so, yet through hardship and pain, Salvis would remain faithful and true.

Luke was especially aware that the King had heard their praises tonight, and he cried out in a loud voice,

"The battle goes on! Salvis has promised never to forsake us! Whatever happens, we won't be alone!"

Rosie, sitting next to him muttered, "He thinks that he's like Morwen now!"

Chapter 9

To Prosper or to Harm

Raldi the carpenter was uneasy. This meeting he had been asked to attend was about making drastic changes to the way of life on Karensa.

This was the first time that Raldi had been to the far side of the island and he did not like the place.

The countryside was gentle and warm – far more beautiful than the farming land he had left behind – so there was no logical reason to dislike the town.

It was a pleasant place. The houses were neat, with white painted walls and tubs of flowers outside each door. Windows were brightly curtained and everywhere was very clean; even the cobbles in the streets shone!

People here were kind and there was nothing he could see to cause his unease, but something disturbed Raldi.

In the town no-one mentioned the King, although Raldi knew that many people who lived here kept the King's law. These people never voiced their opinion and seemed content to be told what to do by the Guardians.

And the Guardians certainly ruled with power!

A new army building had been erected right in the centre of the town and the Guardian's presence was formidable. Dark blue and grey uniforms could be seen at every street corner.

They still wore the hated silver serpent on their tunics and shields. Raldi could never look at the serpents without feeling a great sadness and also a pang of shame because it reminded him of the time when he had betrayed his belief in the King and worn the emblem of Lord Bellum's power himself.

People seemed unaware that the Guardians were Bellum's men. No matter whom the leader might be, Tomas or Hawk, they served the King's enemy.

Rolf and Hawk had invited Raldi to the meeting in the Guardians Hall.

Hawk was the young leader who had replaced Tomas who had been sent away in disgrace.

Rolf was a new man about who little was known, but Raldi decided that since he had befriended the children, he must be on the King's side.

From his seat at the head of the long, polished table, Hawk was smiling amiably. Hawk often smiled, but his eyes never smiled at the same time as his mouth.

Raldi was unsure of this man even though he offered friendship. Hawk's straight hair and thin face reminded Raldi of the boy, Jay, who was living at Petroc's farm. Hawk could hardly be more than twenty years old, so it could be that he and Jay were brothers?

But Jay followed the King, which was why he had been forced to flee to the farmland on the near side of the island. Raldi's thoughts raced. Maybe Jay was a spy for the Guardians? Or maybe Hawk secretly followed the King? Raldi did not think so.

Hawk was speaking now and still smiling. "Friends, you have heard my proposal. What is your response? Shall we work as one?"

Rolf supported him. "As for me, I say yes. Your plans are good plans, Hawk. They will prosper Karensa. There is nothing in them to harm anyone providing the people of the fisher village and farms are left free to follow the ways of the King."

Hawk nodded his agreement. "That decision will be left to our friend Raldi. He is leader of the village council. What he allows or forbids will be for him to decide. Myself, I would advise against it, for the ways of the King's people will surely bring unrest to others. However it is for Raldi to decide."

Raldi's unease grew. He knew that he should defend the King's people and deny they caused trouble, but he was outnumbered and he said nothing.

The other men waited expectantly but still he hesitated. He did not like what he saw of Hawk and he could not make up his mind about Rolf, either. Rolf made Raldi think of Lord Salvis. Raldi had never actually seen Salvis, but Rolf said things that Raldi would expect the King's son to say.

Another thought crept into his mind, unbidden and unexpected. *'It is my plans which will prosper not harm you, my plans alone.'*

Raldi knew those were words the King would say and they seemed to agree with Hawk and Rolf. If the King approved, this must surely be the right way to go.

If Raldi had listened more carefully to the King's words he would not have agreed so quickly.

'...my plans alone'.

Raldi was not listening correctly to his thought. Rolf's plan had not come from the King but from those who were not the King's followers.

Those people were still looking for a decision.

"On condition my people are free to follow the ways of the King, I will support this plan," he said firmly

Each leader in turn signed the document. From now on, Hawk would send enough Guardians to enforce law and order in the fisher village and farms where they could deal with the unrest caused by the young people. The fisher village had previously sent them away, but this time things were different.

Raldi would govern the fisher village and farms. Hawk would govern the far side of the island. Both would answer to one leader; Rolf.

Karensa was now a Military State.

Morwen needed supplies and Luke had gone with her to the Fisher Village. They were buying wool to make new blankets which were now popular bedding, replacing furs. As she paid for her purchases, Rolf and Raldi rode into the village square followed by a troop of Guardians.

Every head turned as the two leaders mounted the very same platform where Petroc had died. The Guardians spread out around the platform, swords ready. Wisely, they not longer wore the serpent on their shields.

One by one, villagers left shops and houses and for the most part, they stood in silence, No-one thought to see Guardians here again, nor wanted them.

Raldi held up his hand for silence, but there was no need because no-one was speaking.

"Friends, I understand your fears." he said. His voice echoed eerily around the silent square. "You have cause to dislike the Guardians, as indeed have I. But things are different now. Tomas has gone. A younger leader has taken his place. There is no cause for concern. These soldiers are here to help us and I myself shall command them. This day we have come to an agreement which will change our lives for the better." He paused for effect, then with hands held high he proclaimed, "Karensa is now one State! We have one ruler who will take care of both sides of the island. This man will bring peace and prosperity to Karensa such as we have never known before. And here is this man!"

Rolf stepped forward and stood next to Raldi. He was greeted with a ripple of interest. Rolf was a good man. He had helped them many times. They could not have chosen a better leader. They could trust Rolf. They would be safe under his rule.

The people clapped and then shouted their approval.

"Who is there like Rolf? We will serve him well!"

"He has my support!"

"Rolf deserves this!"

"Who can make war against Rolf the Good?"

Others took this up until the village square resounded with their thunderous chant.

"Who is like Rolf? Who is like Rolf? Who is like Rolf?"

Then Rolf cried in a loud voice, "Long Live the Island State of Karensa!"

Morwen looked away. "It is time we went home," she said wearily and her tone of voice told Luke not to argue, even though he was curious to know what the people would do next. The scene brought back painful memories of the last time they had seen the brother and friend they loved.

"We shall take the coastal path. It is faster," she said, as though she could not wait to get away from the village, but as soon as they reached a grassy spot she threw her basket to one side and sat down.

Luke followed her. The grass smelt of the coming Time of Plenty, of sun and bees and flowers; good things, not soldiers in uniforms.

Morwen burst into tears. Covering her face with her hands she sobbed as though her heart would break.

Luke felt helpless. He had no idea what to do. Clumsily, he held her until her sobs subsided.

At last she dried her eyes on the sleeve of her tunic. "I never thought to see the Guardians again, not after…

Petroc died to get rid of them and he may as well not have bothered for they are back. The battle never ends, Luke. It never ends!"

Luke searched for the right words. "It won't be the same. Raldi is still in control..."

"Raldi has turned sides before!"

"But there is Rolf as well. Rolf makes me feel... I don't know... safe I suppose. He would never harm us."

Morwen sighed deeply. "I know but... it was seeing them again with their blue cloaks and swords. We don't need them here. The King's law is enough."

It seemed to Luke that the people wanted Rolf, not the King's law. It could be worse. At least Rolf was kind and would look after them. Yet hearts had grown cold towards the King and towards each other.

So why did Rolf so trouble the peace in his heart?

Slowly, solemnly, the doors of the Royal palace swung open. In the Great Hall, where stood the Three Thrones, the King's servants knelt to greet the new arrival.

With majesty and purpose, the white horse entered the Palace, his silver mane and tail swishing from side to side and his head held proud and high. As he approached the Thrones, the silence was shattered by a shout of acclamation.

"The time of deliverance is near!"

The doors closed. The horse took up his position beside the Three Thrones, there to wait patiently with the King and his Son and the Unseen Lord, until the day when Lord Salvis would ride out to take back the Lost Kingdom

Chapter 10

A Time of Peace

"The Time of Plenty will soon be here," Rosie observed.

After supper she and Luke had walked down to the farm gate. On their first visit to Karensa, the King himself had sent them to this farm where he knew they would be well cared for. The farmer and his wife, Tobias and Martha, had treated them as their own, but the farm gate had always been their special place to talk about home and things only they could understand.

"It will soon be warm enough to swim," Luke added.

"Maybe we shall swim with the dolphins again. We haven't seen them since we came back… I never thought we would come to Karensa again, not after last time."

She sounded so sad that Luke said, "I know you didn't really want to come."

"I didn't," Rosie admitted. "I still don't want to be here, but things… things haven't been so bad since Karensa became a State. Rolf is a good man who makes a strong leader. He looks after us."

"It's early days yet," Luke replied thoughtfully.

Luke had yet to be convinced that Rolf was the best thing for the island. His sister looked puzzled, so he tried his best to explain.

"The King's people are free, but no-one really likes them, especially not me and you. They don't want to hear about the King or Salvis and never come to the praise meetings at the farm. They talk about Rolf as though he is a king. They chant '*who is like Rolf*' and Rolf loves it!"

"Rolf is our friend," Rosie protested. "He talks to us like Salvis did when we lived in the Bay of Dolphins."

Rosie desired to feel safe and happy. Why did her brother have to make things so complicated? There had been sorrow enough on the island.

But Luke replied, "No-one ever speaks like Salvis. Rolf spends time with us and he helps us, but that's because he wants to be friends with everybody."

Rosie gazed across to the Dark Forest, each tree holding high its branches to welcome the coming night. Owls hooted softly and bats fluttered crazily in the dusk. It was peaceful here.

Rosie decided that her brother was wrong this time. The new Government really had brought peace to the island and the King's people and the Guardians lived side by side in harmony, no longer wearing the emblems of service to Bellum. Rosie felt secure and now Luke had spoilt things.

And her brother was nowhere near finishing sharing his unwelcome thoughts. It seemed as though someone had wound him up and he couldn't stop.

"Rolf's started something he calls the Time of Decisions like the King used to do when people could still enter the Royal Palace. Rolf makes judgements, just like the King used to do."

Rosie chewed on her bottom lip. She had heard of this and truly it made her uncomfortable inside because no-one could ever take the place of the King.

"Rolf gives the people food, just like the King used to," Luke went on angrily. "Where does he get the food from, I want to know. Not from the King."

"Where is it from then?" Rosie murmured. It was ages since her brother had lost his temper and it still worried her a little.

"There's only one person it could come from." Luke replied meaningfully.

"Not from Bellum?" Rosie shuddered. Lord Bellum was hardly ever seen nowadays. It was a though he wanted to be forgotten.

"Who else would it be? He doesn't own farm land and takes no taxes from the people. We know the King would never help the Guardians, no matter how friendly they seem. Rolf never turns anyone away. He just gives the hungry the food they need. Where does he get the food?"

Rosie's secure, comfortable feeling crumbled. "You said you liked Rolf," she whispered lamely.

"Well yes, I do," her brother admitted. "What's not to like? I wish I could think who he reminds me of, though. It's at the back of my mind, all the time."

"Maybe… maybe Rolf is just trying to help people the best way he knows how? Children don't come now from the far side of the island, so things must be better there? The Guardians are led by Jay's brother. He can't be as bad as Tomas, surely?"

Luke wished he could agree with her. "Jay and his brother don't get on," he replied. "Anyway, it's getting dark. We're having a praise meeting tonight. At least Rolf allows us to still praise the King. Let's go inside."

Rosie slipped her arm through his and as they walked home together, they both tried to put aside the niggling fear in their hearts.

While they were praising the King at Petroc's farm, Lord Rolf opened his doors to the people so they might come to him with their problems.

He was seated on a wooden, throne-like chair of office at one end of a long, low room. This house had once belonged to Esram's Uncle Carrik in the days before he became a King's man. In those days, Carrik had served Lord Bellum.

The Guardians formed two lines on either side of the room, making a guard of honour for their leader. Raldi sat on a smaller chair, behind Rolf.

Both men had changed greatly. Rolf now wore a cloak of purple and a circlet of jewels covered his hair. He held his head high as though aware of his importance, yet his eyes were gentle and his expression kindly so that none could be afraid.

Raldi was no longer a simple carpenter. Now he wore the new Guardian uniform which was grey and dark blue, but without the hated serpent emblazoned on the tunic. Around his neck was a heavy golden chain of office.

Rolf stood up. "Admit my people!" he cried in a loud voice. "Raldi, draw the sword of justice! Let the Time of Decisions commence!"

The people of Karensa filed into the hall and one by one presented their requests; food or medicine or help to repair a boat or money to buy shoes for growing children. Every person was treated politely and every request granted except one.

A certain man known to be loyal to the King was told that he must dig his own land even though he had injured his back. Rolf suggested that maybe the King would heal the pain in his back so that he could do his own work. However, although his request was denied, Rolf still treated him with respect and reprimanded those who laughed at him behind their hands when help had been refused.

Just as Lord Rolf was about to close the Time of Decisions, a small group of ragged men came in and bowed before Rolf and Raldi.

A grey haired man was their spokesman. "My name is Hathan, Lord Rolf. I am a fishing man."

Rolf nodded, hiding his impatience. He was hungry and wanted the Decision Time to end.

"State your request, friend Hathan."

Hathan was clearly nervous. "My lord, now that Karensa is one State, things go well with us. You have indeed met our every need. We are at peace. Yet there are still those who stubbornly serve the King."

"That is so. As long as they do not come to my Government for help and keep their ideas to themselves, it is not a problem. All should be free to choose. They are my people just as you are my people."

"Yes lord, but are they content with this? They insist on spreading their lies abroad. My own children came home one day with a ridiculous story about Lord Salvis still being alive. This was told them by other children who still serve the King. These people need to be stopped. They will spoil all that we have achieved."

"I would not allow that to happen," Rolf said cautiously. "Neither would Raldi. You need not fear this. Just tell your children the truth."

Raldi, who was secretly still a King's man, looked uncomfortable. He thought about the family at Petroc's farm, but he did not speak up for them.

Hathan pressed in. "Now they have heard this story, they will not listen to me! We do better without the King! Oh yes, I once was deceived, but no more! What has the King ever done to help me?"

"What would you have us do?" asked Rolf slowly.

Hathan became bold. "My lord, we would ask that those who serve the King have their property taken away from them. Further more, we ask that any visitors to the island be arrested for they would seem to be the root of these lies."

Raldi's face was troubled. He would never wish the family of Petroc any harm.

"If we refuse your request, what then?" he asked.

"If you refuse," Hathan's voice deepened in a menacing way. "Well then, Raldi, we would question your loyalty to the State. "

His friends murmured their agreement but Rolf was not going to fall into the trap of mistrusting those who served him.

"We shall cast our votes on this," he said firmly. "That is the democratic way."

So a vote was taken and the new law was passed.

Rolf's voice was heavy. "Friend, your request is granted. Raldi, I appoint you to see this done. All who follow the King must lose their property, be it large or small. All visitors must be arrested and taken to the prison in the fisher village where they can do no further harm. They will be fed and cared for, but not be able to deceive others with their lies. Act quickly. Your first call must be Petroc's farm."

Raldi's heart sank. He hung his head. "Oh my lord, I cannot… this family were always my friends…"

"It is the will of the people and for the good of the state," Rolf reminded him in a gentle voice which said that he understood.

Raldi groaned. "For Karensa and the good of the people, I will obey. The deed shall be done this night… Where is the man who came for help and was refused?"

This man was trying to slip out without being seen but he was seized and arrested.

Raldi told himself that no real harm would come to his friends and that the King would understand that he acted for the good of all people.

Chapter 11

Enemies of the State

Once again their old friends had not come to the praise meeting. Only household members were there. Not to be deterred, they sang loudly to make up for empty seats.

Esram led the meeting because Martha preferred to sit quietly with her own thoughts. Esram asked the King to send help to them from the Royal Palace. At first they might as well have been singing to the kitchen wall.

Then, quite suddenly it was as though Salvis himself was there.

They couldn't see him, but they knew he was there. No-one spoke. Time seemed to stand still. A minute could have passed, or it might have been an hour.

During this wonderful time, Morwen walked to the front of the room. She was trembling so much that Esram had to steady her.

"I believe Lord Salvis has something to say to us," she told them. "Oh, he has shown me a terrible picture! He says the testing time is here! There will be danger for us all! He says we are not to fear, that he will never leave us!" Morwen covered her face with her hands to stop the tears streaming down her cheeks. "I do not want to bring such a message, but I believe the King is preparing us." Her voice then became stronger. "The King says that time is short and soon the day of the White Horse will be upon us. Salvis returns soon! Salvis returns very soon!"

In the stunned silence, Esram helped Morwen to sit down and Luke and Rosie stood very close together.

Holly came beside them and whispered, "Morwen has done this before and never once been wrong. I... I'm so afraid..."

Luke put his free arm around Holly and she put hers around Jay, and the young people supported each other until the meeting was brought to an abrupt halt by a loud banging on the door.

Esram sighed with relief. "All is well! It is the Guardians, but Raldi is with them. Raldi, we have not seen you for so long. How have you been?"

Rosie whispered to Luke, "Remember the night they took Salvis away? We thought we were safe then because Josh was with the soldiers. We didn't know that Josh had betrayed us. This could be the same sort of thing."

That very same thought had occurred to her brother and they held on tightly to each other, fearing the worst.

"I have been busy," was Raldi's curt reply to Esram.

It was plain that past friendship with Raldi would count for nothing. He was a Guardian now. They stood close together, just a few young people with no power of their own standing against the might of the State.

"We have come to ask you to make your choice," Raldi told them sternly. "There is no longer a place on Karensa for those who follow the King. You must also surrender your visitors for they are trouble makers. Then you must forget these stories about Salvis and the King."

Esram did not hesitate. "Visitors - why don't you call them by their names? There are no other visitors to the island except Luke and Rosie. You know we will never surrender them or forsake the King, the true and rightful ruler of Karensa. When Morwen and I are married, such decisions will be mine to take and I know that even now, she will honour them?"

Morwen's green eyes were gentle but her voice was firm and strong.

"Esram, I honour your decision. It is the decision my brother Petroc would have made. It is mine too… Raldi, you are our oldest friend. Do you come against us now? Soon, Salvis will ride from the Royal Palace to claim back Karensa for the King. What shall you say to Salvis when you have to look into his eyes?"

Rather than soften Raldi, these words convicted him of his own weakness and he spoke more harshly.

"I will give you children one last chance. Pledge loyalty to the State of Karensa. Surrender your visitors!"

"No," Esram declared. "We will not forsake the King. We will not surrender our friends."

It was at this point that Martha, overcoming the pain in her joints, struggled to the door. Her voice every bit as firm as her daughter's.

"Do you dare to suggest such a thing, Raldi? My husband and my son gave their lives rather than betray the King! How can you imagine we would forsake him?"

Without further ado, Raldi gave the order to his men to arrest the visitors. They crashed into the house, pushing Martha to one side. Two Guardians seized Luke while others roughly dragged Rosie outside.

Esram tried to fight them but was knocked to the ground. Jay, smaller and lighter, tried to tackle them and received a kick so hard that for a few moments he couldn't breath.

Luke and Rosie were carried by two horsemen into the Dark Forest. The last thing they heard from the farm was Holly, screaming.

"I cannot believe you are doing this to us, Raldi," said Martha, regarding the small bundle of possessions they had been allowed to gather together.

Raldi's face was expressionless. "Martha, all you need to do to stop this, is to pledge support to the State."

"We cannot do that," Esram replied. His heart was thudding loudly. "The family of Tobias and Petroc will always belong to the King."

"Not for much longer," Raldi said, but now his voice sounded sad.

He nodded to his men and Holly screamed. She was not the sort of person to scream and cry but this treatment was unbelievably cruel.

They watched helplessly as their home was smashed apart. Rugs and cushions that had been made with love were ripped and thrown into the mud and trampled by soldier's boots. Chairs were splintered by soldier's swords. Pots and pans were tossed out of the windows. Worst of all, Martha's bed which Raldi had fashioned with his own hands, he now chopped into firewood.

When it was over they were told to leave the farm and never return. They were now outlaws. Like Luke and Rosie they were enemies of the State. They could be killed on sight by anyone and that person would go unpunished.

Martha looked long at the spot beneath the cherry tree where Tobias and Petroc were buried.

"How can I leave them?" she sobbed. "How can I go and leave them alone? My husband, my son…"

Morwen and Esram comforted her.

"Mother, you know only their remains lie there," Morwen said tearfully. "Their spirits are far away, with Salvis in the Royal Palace."

"I know daughter, I know. They are at peace now and past their pain. Where as we…"

"We continue to fight!" It was Jay who unexpectedly restored their hope. "We have lost one battle, not the war.

The battle belongs to the King and he will have the final victory."

"You will get the farm back, one day," said Holly. "The King will not let them take it away from you forever."

"No," said Martha sadly. "We will not return. I sense it in my spirit. Petroc fought so hard for this farm and now we have lost it. Oh, Salvis, how long shall you be? How long before you return?"

"Not long, Mother," Morwen whispered. "Remember what the King said to us in the meeting. Salvis is coming soon! The white horse is coming soon!"

So with dignity, the family left their ruined home.

Beyond High Hill was a grove of trees and here they took shelter.

Morwen made her mother as comfortable as possible on a bed of ferns. They would be safe here for the night. The grove was well hidden.

When Martha was settled, Morwen sat down and Esram knelt by her side.

"We cannot abandon Luke and Rosie. At least we can ask the King to help them," Morwen said.

"That's what we must do," Esram agreed. "Let's ask quietly, each speaking from their heart. Even without saying the words out loud, the King will hear us."

As they pleaded silently, the grove became still and so deep were their thoughts that they did not hear Rolf join them.

Jay saw him first but all he could do was to open and close his mouth. Rolf was the supreme ruler of the State. They were now enemies of the State. Why should Rolf come here?

"Peace, all of you," said Rolf softly. "Don't fear me for I am your friend. I do not approve of what has been done this day."

"Then why did you let it happen?" cried Holly, who was never short of words.

"My children, I had no choice," Rolf explained sadly. "Karensa is now a democracy and the people voted for this law. I must maintain peace on the island but I will help you in any way I can."

"Then set our friends free!" Holly exclaimed.

"Child, I cannot do that, but I can promise they will come to no real harm. You are in danger if you stay here. The people are angry with the King's followers. You are outlaws."

"Where can we go then, Rolf?" Morwen's voice was subdued, almost as though she was pondering.

Rolf would have touched her arm, but for reasons she could not explain, Morwen pulled away.

Esram saw it and moved between them. He would always protect Morwen. Once, a long time ago, he had risked his own life to rescue her. His love for her grew stronger every day.

The light returned to Martha's eyes and she made a decision.

"We will go to the place that gave us shelter before, the place where Salvis taught and guided us."

Morwen gave a sharp intake of breath. "Why didn't I think of it? You mean the Bay of Dolphins! We will go to the Bay of Dolphins!"

Chapter 12

A Place of Safety

"You must travel during the night," Rolf urged. "Most people respect the curfew and stay at home after dark so you will not be seen."

"Will you come with us, Rolf?" Holly asked with unusual fearfulness.

"I cannot, child. The Guardians will notice my absence. They must not suspect I am helping you."

He left as quickly as he had arrived. Afterwards Esram and Morwen shared the same thought. The Bay of Dolphins was a long way. How could Martha manage such a journey?

The older lady must have guessed what they were thinking.

"Morwen, you are all I have left of my family. Do not put yourself at risk because of me. Leave me here."

Her daughter replied fiercely, "That we shall never do!"

"You will not have to!"

A strange voice startled them all, but their fear was unfounded for this stranger was never more welcome.

"Lord Veritan!" Morwen exclaimed. "Oh, I knew the King would not desert us. He has sent you to help us!"

Veritan confirmed this by inclining his head, his silver hair gleaming in the light of the quarter moon. He stretched out his arm so that his shadow hovered over them until they were comforted and their failing hearts were hopeful again.

"May the King bless this little household," he said finally. "May Lord Salvis uphold each of you. Always remember that the King is no more than a heart's cry away."

Esram started to ask about Luke and Rosie but even as he spoke, Veritan vanished.

Jay helped a shaken Holly to her feet and the others followed. In that grove beyond High Hill, joy stirred in their hearts as they received through Veritan, the peace of being protected by the King.

"Come," said Martha resolutely, "we have many miles to cover this night. Before we see the bright morning star of dawn, we must reach the Bay of Dolphins."

Fear and the stale air inside the cell made them both feel sick. Rosie clung tightly to her brother. There was something she desperately needed to ask. It was upsetting but she felt she must say it.

"This isn't... I mean... this is not where Petroc..."

"No," Luke replied very quickly. "The room where they kept Petroc was clean and had a proper bed. It had a window too. It was upstairs, I think... This... this is a dungeon. They must really hate us."

Under guard they had been taken to the prison in the fisher village and once there, down a flight of slippery winding stairs.

It really was a dungeon. It had no window. A torch made from rushes revealed cold, damp stone walls. A pile of dirty straw in one corner was their bed. They had nothing to eat or drink. They could be left here to starve.

Suddenly Luke was very, very tired. He separated himself from Rosie. "It must be late. I know we shan't sleep, but let's try."

They snuggled into the straw to keep warm and Luke was wrong for they were so exhausted that they both slept, at least for a little while.

Luke awoke with a start. He had been dreaming the dream that he had before they ever came to Karensa.

In the dream he was very young, and Mum was pushing him on the garden swing. Rosie, a baby, played in the sandpit. The swing went higher and higher and his mother was saying, *"Find the place, Luke, the place where dolphins race with rainbows…"*

Now they had found that place - it was Karensa - yet his mum was still calling to him.

Why, and why now?

It had been years since Luke had cried, but now he cried in secret, cried for his mum, for Petroc, for Salvis, but most of all because he was afraid and he knew there was no way out of here. They may never see Dad or Stacey again.

Once he gave way to his tears, it was as though a tap had been turned on in his heart.

Rosie woke up and now it was her turn to help him. He was ashamed of his own weakness.

"I brought you here," he said brokenly. "I talked you into coming. You didn't want to. It was my fault again. It's always me! I always have to know best!"

"It wasn't like that. We had to come. It's all about the white horse, Luke. It's about Salvis coming back soon. And… and you are wrong about them hating us. When they see us it reminds them they should be loyal to the King. It's themselves they hate, not us."

With that profound revelation, she determinedly closed her mind to the very real danger they were in. Rosie had never thought of herself as brave but she resolved not to think about what the Guardians had done to Petroc.

"Hey, let's talk about what we're going to do when we leave school? I'm really working on my music. I want to write songs and sing them for the Great King."

Luke wiped his face with his sleeve and gamely tried to follow her lead.

"I still want to go abroad," he admitted. "Maybe I shall go to Bible School. I'd like to do missionary work."

"We both want to serve the Great King," Rosie said thoughtfully. "We learn a lot about him while we're on Karensa. Every time we come back here we seem to learn more. I don't think it was a mistake coming back. I think it was meant to be. We shall get out of this place, Luke. I know we shall. The King will make a way."

"He'll make a way where there seems to be no way," he replied wryly, then explained. "That's in the Bible. I'll show you when we get home."

He did not add that unless the King intervened, going home was not an option.

The dawn sun crept from behind the mist just as they reached the Bay of Dolphins.

At the top of the cliffs they paused to look over this vast bay where silver waves lapped against the sand and gulls swept low over the gold–tinged rocks. The day promised to be fair but they were all too tired to think of anything but finding a place to rest.

Wearily, Morwen led them down to the beach, then up some steps leading to a house built into a cave, high on the cliff. She could not speak. This place rekindled so many sweet memories of love and friendship, because they had lived in this house for almost a year.

It was here that Salvis had taught them and healed them and it was on this beach they first saw him when he lived again having once died. Even now at this terrible time, she still sensed the peace he had brought. It was all around them, as real as the sea birds circling overhead.

Oh, so many memories! In her mind she saw two children, herself and Luke, being brought to this cave by a man called Kett, who had built the cave house. It was just before the Time of Snows and it was bitterly cold. Now, like so many friends, Kett was dead.

Morwen and Luke had been close friends then and once they had both secretly believed they would spend their lives together when they grew up. But later, Morwen grew to love Esram and knew he was the one she wanted for her own.

Yet Luke would always be special. Where was he now? Rosie would be afraid. Where had the Guardians taken them and what would they do to them?

When she opened the door of the cave house she was even more confused. The house should have been in ruins, but it was very much as they had left it when they went home again, all those years ago. The table, the benches, the few pots and pans they left behind looked as though someone had cleaned them in readiness for their arrival today.

Jay and Holly were fascinated by the house built into a cave and could not resist touching everything.

Morwen watched and smiled at them until Esram interrupted her.

"Your mother needs to rest," he said quietly. "Do not be alarmed, but the journey was hard for her. We all need to sleep."

For the first time ever, Morwen turned her face away from him. He could not understand how she was feeling. He had no memories of this place.

She helped Martha to a bed of dried seaweed and covered her with her own cloak.

Martha gave her a beautiful smile.

"Morwen, I could not have asked for a better daughter than you have been. I have been greatly blessed by you, my child. You have comforted me and cared for me when your own heart was breaking. Be a good wife to Esram and mother to his children."

They left Martha to sleep and went outside to scour the beach for fuel before the rest of the island awoke.

Suddenly, Morwen lifted her head from her work and ran back to the cave house.

Her mother was just as they had left her, one thin hand tucked beneath her chin. Her face was peaceful. The pain had gone and the years had slipped away and Martha looked young again.

Morwen knelt by her side and softly touched her cheek. It was cold. She had left them. She had slipped away, gently and quietly, in her sleep.

Chapter 13

Sing for your Supper

Jay and Holly were sitting by a window overlooking the beach. The day was going to be warm and sunny. Even at this early hour, the sky was clear and blue, lazy waves lapped against the shore. This day was given for joy, not sorrow.

"To look out there," said Holly, speaking quietly so as not to disturb the sleeping Morwen, "you would not think there was any trouble at all."

"We left the far side of the island to escape trouble," said Jay. "Maybe you can't really escape things because we seem worse off here!"

"I'm so scared for Luke and Rosie. Rolf promised they would be safe, but –"

"– we don't know if we can trust him," Jay finished.

"He reminds a lot of people of Salvis. He could be a friend of Salvis. He could be working for the Guardians so he can help the King's people in secret."

Jay did not answer, and Holly's attention turned to Morwen.

"I have never seen so many tears as Morwen has cried."

"Her mother has died!" Jay protested.

"I know, but…" Holly couldn't find the words to explain her feelings. They all looked to Morwen for encouragement. Holly was not hard of heart. She found it upsetting to see her friend distressed.

"I miss Martha too," she whispered. "Jay, will you give me a hug, please?"

Jay had never actually been asked to hug someone before but he obliged and found that he quite liked it. He was almost sorry when she pulled away, sniffing loudly and saying they needed to find drinking water.

They found an empty cooking pot and filled it from a clear stream which trickled down the cliff on to the beach. They had nothing to eat, but were too sad to be hungry.

To make sure that their hiding place would not be discovered, they remained in the cave house until dusk. Then, as the boys went out to catch crabs, they saw a man in the Bay of Dolphins. The man left a package by the cliff path, then waved and went on his way.

Esram and Jay raced to see what the man had left behind and found food and blankets.

"It must have been Rolf," said Jay and Esram agreed because no-one else knew they were there except Rolf and Veritan and the figure was too small for a Lord of the Palace. Surely this was proof of Rolf's friendship?

After dark, the boys took a spade from the back of the cave house and in a sheltered spot overlooking the bay, they laid Martha to rest.

"She would like it here," said Morwen. "She would sooner lie with Father and Petroc, but that cannot be. This is the next best place for her. Once, we were all very happy here."

"She does not have to lie with Tobias and Petroc for her spirit to be with them," Esram reminded her.

Holly added, "Luke said that once he was given a glimpse inside the Royal Palace and he saw Petroc there and I believe him."

"That's where they will really be," Jay agreed.

Morwen trusted them and she trusted Luke. She had never known him to tell lies. It got him into trouble sometimes but she respected him for it.

She was content to know that her mother was now past all pain and was living at peace with Salvis and the King.

Rosie tried hard to forget how hungry she was. They had no way of knowing how long they had been here. The torch on the wall was burning low. Rosie dare not think what it would be like when it was completely dark.

"Somebody must come soon," said Luke optimistically. His throat was dry and his voice cracked because they were desperately thirsty.

"I'm bored," Rosie replied. It wasn't true. She was too scared to be bored.

This irritated her brother. "If you had never bought that jigsaw, we wouldn't be here!" he snapped with a flash of his old temper.

"If you hadn't lost one piece, we wouldn't be here!"

"I didn't lose it. You did!"

"You found the stairs! You made me go up them!"

They stared at each other, two dirty, frightened children very aware of the danger they were in.

"We shouldn't argue," Luke said at last. "It wasn't anybody's fault we are here. We just are. It –"

With a creak, the cell door swung open. Two Guardians stood there.

"You are honoured," said one. "You are going to the highest power on Karensa."

"Are we going to the King?" Rosie asked hopefully.

The man spat. "What King? You, maiden, are going to see Lord Bellum!"

"No!" Luke moved between Rosie and the guards. "Take me to Bellum instead. Take me, not Rosie!"

The two soldiers did not trouble to reply. One of them brought down the flat of his sword on Luke's shoulder. He never knew what hit him.

Rosie shrank back into the cell. That made them angry.

"We don't want to come into this stinking place!" one of them shouted.

In no time at all, Rosie was dragged away and by the time Luke staggered to his feet, he was alone. He banged on the cell door but that only bruised his hands.

Lord Bellum's castle was even more sinister than Rosie remembered. Morwen had once called it a castle of shadows. It towered against the sky, darker than the darkest night.

She was taken to a big hall where Lord Bellum himself sat on a throne, beneath a canopy of black velvet. The walls were hung with rich tapestries but Rosie knew the splendour meant nothing. This was a place of shadows, of darkness and evil.

Rosie was forced to kneel before Bellum's throne. She tried to focus her thoughts on Lord Salvis. She held on to a picture of his kind face and the memory of his gentle voice and that helped her.

Bellum lifted his hand so that emeralds and rubies sparkled from his fingers. Rosie had forgotten how handsome he was, with his black hair and pale skin and dark eyes. Dressed in a scarlet tunic and a cloak of gold, trimmed with jewels, he was truly magnificent.

"The child may stand."

Her guards hauled her to her feet and Lord Bellum continued to scrutinise her.

"Unloose her hair," Bellum ordered.

Rosie hand went to her plaits but before she had time to protest, her thick, fair hair hung down in loose curls.

Bellum smiled lazily. "You see, Rosie, you are as lovely as Morwen was when she came here." *

*   *Castle of Shadows*

Rosie forced herself to speak, trying to hide her fear.

"It was Morwen's own decision to come here that day," she protested bravely. "I was forced here."

"Whatever," the dark haired lord shrugged. "How you came does not matter. You are here."

Rosie's curiosity made her bold. "Why? Why did you have me brought here?"

Right at that moment, Rosie's stomach rumbled. Bellum laughed at her.

"You are hungry then, Rosie?"

"You know I am! We haven't been fed!"

Bellum clapped his hands and at once servants hurried in carrying plates of food; meat and fruit and new baked bread. They held the tempting display just beyond her reach. Her stomach growled. The smell of the food made her feel dizzy.

"Then eat," Bellum told her, but as her hand reached out he placed his black sword in front of the food.

"Ah no, there is something you must do first, Rosie; only a little thing. I heard you sing once in the Dark Forest. Oh, you did not know I was there, but I heard you. Sing for us now, Rosie. Sing for your supper! Then you shall stay here and be my songster and your brother will be held in a better place and given food and water."

Rosie felt faint and tried to be brave. She started to sing, her voice no less lovely for want of water. The only song she could think of was the one she had written herself.

"Innocent one, gentle and meek,
Friend of the poor, friend of the weak,
Live in my heart today…
You live in my heart today…"

Then, the same thing happened as when she sang at the praise meeting; the notes were the same, but the words were special ones given by the King. They rose and fell, rose and fell and resounded around the hall, a song of victory, unknown words about a love that conquers all.

Her song ended abruptly when Bellum's hand made contact with her cheek. Rosie fell to the floor, sobbing wildly. Bellum's dark eyes glinted with amber lights and that meant that he was very angry.

"How did you learn those words? You will regret singing them to me!"

Lord Bellum had not understood her song, but he knew she was singing about Salvis and he knew that the special words came from the King.

"Guards - return her to her brother in the dung she came from! Give them nothing to eat or drink. They can stay there until they rot!"

The guards took hold of her. They were rough but to her astonishment one of them, a tall, quiet man, secretly placed a small flask of water inside her cloak.

Wonderingly, Rosie looked into the man's eyes and saw compassion.

"I hope you find Salvis for yourself," she whispered.

The guard nodded but he treated her no less roughly than his companion.

Someone had replaced the burnt down torch with a new one, so there was light in the cell when Rosie returned. After sharing her water, she saw that her brother's head was still bleeding

"Never mind that," he told her. "You're back and we're together again, even if we are in here. What did Bellum want with you?"

"I sang for him, only... he didn't like what I sang."

"What didn't he like?"

Rosie grinned and then she sang in her special words and Luke joined in.

Singing made them stronger. They were still singing when the cell door creaked open.

They feared the worst, but it was the tall guard who had shown Rosie kindness. Now he brought them food. It was only bread and cheese yet it was the most wonderful food they had ever tasted.

"Are you ready to go now?" asked the guard when they had eaten the last crumb. His voice sounded familiar. Beneath his helmet they glimpsed silver hair and at his side was a golden sword.

"It's Lord Veritan again!" Luke breathed.

"He keeps popping up!" Rosie added unnecessarily.

The King had not forsaken them. All they needed to do was to trust him.

Chapter 14

Time is Running out

Luke and Rosie stared in disbelief.

"Don't you want to leave?" Veritan asked.

"How can we?" squeaked Rosie.

Luke added, "There are Guardians everywhere."

"What are a few Guardians compared to the power of the King? Don't you trust him? Don't you trust me? Will you not put your lives in my hands, even now?"

They both nodded, feeling a little ashamed.

"Then follow me and prepare to be surprised."

Heart pounding, they crept out of the cell and up the slippery stone steps, expecting to be stopped by Guardians at any second. It did not happen.

The night air was ever so sweet in that first moment of freedom.

"There were loads of soldiers everywhere. Where have they gone?" Rosie wondered.

"Ah well," said Veritan mysteriously, "you must learn to trust your King.

They hurried on in silence and when they reached the Dark Forest, Veritan whistled softly and from a thicket came his grey horse, followed by a horse which was smaller and brown.

"We can't ride!" Rosie cried in dismay.

"I shall lead the horse for you," Lord Veritan promised.

It was unwise to argue with a Lord of the Palace, even if he was on your side, but Luke was wary of horses.

"It's ok, I'll just walk," he declared.

Veritan laughed. "Very well, but it is a very long way to the Bay of Dolphins."

Luke and Rosie were puzzled. Why would they want to go the Bay of Dolphins?

"I will explain as we ride. We are wasting time and the Guardians will return shortly. Rosie, you sit with me on my horse. Luke, you shall ride the brown one."

Luke would never admit to being scared so he clambered onto the horse without showing himself up too much. He told himself that it couldn't be so different from riding a bike but you could tell what a bike was going to do; more or less. Even a steady horse had a mind of its own. Actually, as they started to move, he thought it was cool.

Rosie was glad she was with Veritan. The first day they came to Karensa, she had ridden like this with Veritan to the Royal Palace. Luke had ridden with Lord Bellum, when he was still a friend.

"How did we get out of prison?" she asked. "Where were the Guardians? How did the King know?"

"Maybe he heard the praises you sang? How many times does the King have to help you before you truly trust him?"

The Lord of the Palace sounded sad.

Dawn touched the sky with silver fingers as Morwen ran across the beach to greet them. She hugged Rosie, then Luke and, clinging on desperately, she began to cry.

"We never thought to see you again!" she sobbed into Luke's broad shoulder. "Oh Luke, Rosie...Mother... Mother died. She fell asleep yesterday."

Luke could not trust himself to speak. It was in this exact place that Morwen had learnt of her father's death and then, as now, it was Luke who had comforted her.

They were joined by Esram, Holly and Jay, all looking tired and sad. Holly hugged Rosie who by now was crying too because she had loved Martha. Gently but firmly, Esram took Morwen from Luke and comforted her himself, saying that Luke's sister needed him.

Jay clasped Luke's hand, very formal and polite. "It's good you are here," he said, but his voice trembled ever so slightly.

"It will soon be morning," said Esram. We must stay inside as much as possible during daylight hours to avoid being discovered. We are all outlaws."

He led the way into the cave house. No sooner had the door closed behind them than Rosie burst into tears again, for she remembered so well the time they had lived here and remembered those who had gone; Tobias, Kett, Martha, Petroc.

It still hurt so much when she thought of her friends. Rosie wanted it to hurt. As long as the hurt was there, they still lived in her heart.

Luke went to help his sister but another was there first and without words, they all fell to their knees for it was the only place to be in the presence of the King's son, the wonderful Lord Salvis.

They never knew how long they knelt there but when they got up, the sun was high in the sky. They were content just to be with him.

He had not changed; his dark eyes so kind and his smile so gentle. He still wore the same grey tunic, dark trousers and boots and a cloak of fine blue wool. His light brown hair was still parted in the centre and fell loosely around his oval face.

Finally Salvis spoke. "So, my children, we are together in this place of safety again."

"Shall you stay with us, Lord?" Rosie cried eagerly.

"No, Rosie. My home now is in the Royal Palace until the time comes to finally defeat Bellum."

Rosie sighed. "I wish you could stay, Lord."

"I know you do, but it cannot be."

"Please stay, Lord," pleaded Luke, who never pleaded.

"I cannot." Then Salvis spoke to each of them in turn, telling each one the things they most needed to hear.

"Who are you, Salvis? Who are you really?" asked Luke.

"Luke, you know the answer to that question. You have asked it twice before."

"I need to hear you say it, Lord Salvis."

"No you don't," Salvis replied firmly. "You need faith to believe it."

But to Rosie he said, "When you are ready, I will take away your hurt for Petroc, when you are willing."

"Yes, Salvis," Rosie murmured. "I'm not ready yet."

Salvis nodded. "I know."

Then he was gone and the cave house was empty and cold without him.

Suddenly Luke wondered why no-one had thought to question Salvis about Rolf, but there seemed to be more important things to talk about.

A few days later Holly and Jay took the wild flowers Holly had gathered and placed them where Martha lay sleeping.

"I can't believe we are doing this," Holly said sadly. "We were safe at the farm. Now…"

"Now we live in a cave and we are scared to leave it and Martha is dead and we rely on Rolf for food."

"Rolf will come every few days with fresh supplies. And we are safe enough here. There are only a few scattered farms. And… and I do feel better after talking to Salvis."

"That was the first time I actually saw him," Jay reflected. "He was bigger than I thought."

"What did he say to you?" If Holly wanted to know something, she simply asked.

Jay's pale face turned crimson. Some things were private, even from old friends.

Holly glimpsed a movement in the bushes.

"Jay, we're being watched," she whispered.

"I know. I saw it too."

Quick as a rabbit scurrying down a burrow, Jay threw himself down behind the bush, where he found two small intruders.

They were farm children; a girl of about eight and a younger boy. They both looked scared.

"We meant no harm," the girl whined. "We wondered who was lying here."

Holly and Jay hesitated. These children could be spies.

"It is our friend," Jay said at last. "But it's only her remains really. Her spirit now lives in the Royal Palace with the King."

He felt Holly stiffen.

"Do you know about the King?" the girl asked eagerly. "We want to know about him only no-one will tell us."

"Tell us a story about the King," the boy pleaded.

In spite of Holly's restraining hand on his arm, Jay did not hesitate. One time, they had asked exactly the same question of Esram and he had told them.

Jay explained that Salvis had died to make a way back to the Royal Palace for the people, but now he lives again, only in the Royal Palace. He explained that Salvis was always kind and gentle and forgiving and that anyone could promise to serve him.

The children listened intently then Jay helped them to make that promise. When they went on their way, it was with a new light shining in their eyes.

Holly planted a kiss on Jay's cheek. "I never heard you talk like that before," she explained. "You talked about Salvis in a way I never could. You have changed those children's lives for ever. They will grow up to be content, even when things go wrong."

Doubts crept into Jay's mind.

I am not clever. I am not brave. I could have done that better. Esram would have done it better...

"I made a mess of it. I never even asked their names."

"No, you didn't make a mess of it, Jay! And their names do not matter. The King knows who they are."

Meanwhile, in the Royal Palace, Salvis pleaded again for the people of Karensa. Time was running out.

Excitement gripped the servants of the Palace as they worshipped before the Three Thrones in the Great Hall.

The First Throne of silver was that of the King. The Second Throne of gold belonged to Salvis, with the White Horse standing behind. The Third, rose-coloured Throne, was from where the Unseen Lord sent forth the King's special power.

The Three Thrones were One, and the One was Three. It was the deep mystery of Creation.

The lights from the Thrones, silver, gold and rose, mingled and separated and mingled again. The rose light surrounding the Throne of the Unseen Lord became a crimson fire.

The white horse was no longer content to stand quietly but pawed the ground, anxious to leave.

Preparations were being made for the day when the King's son would ride out of the Palace at the head of a great army; The Day of the White Horse.

Chapter 15

Who is there Like Rolf?

Rolf kept his promise to visit them every few days with food. He no longer hurried away, but sat with them and talked, reassuring them that they would be safe here until it was possible for them to return to the farm. He explained that he was trying to persuade people that the King's followers only desired to live peacefully and that strangers to Karensa were not enemies.

One time, they sat on the beach where the sand was soft and rocks protected them from prying eyes and gave shelter from the sun. The Time of Plenty was unusually hot this year.

Rosie, lying on her back in the sand, looked up at Rolf. Sometimes he reminded her of Salvis, but sometimes he reminded her of someone else only she couldn't think who that person was.

"You must miss Lord Salvis," Rolf said suddenly, as though he almost guessed her thoughts.

Rosie was strangely irritated by this. "We don't miss Salvis, 'cos Salvis is still here," she snapped. "He's here, in our hearts. Don't you feel him, Rolf, in your heart?"

Rolf quickly turned the conversation around.

"Are the provisions I bring enough for you all?"

"Plenty," said Esram, who was still not sure he liked Rolf despite his help. The people's chant *'who is there like Rolf?'* disturbed him, deep inside him where peace should be.

Luke and Esram did not agree about Rolf. Luke maintained that if Rolf was their enemy, he would surely have them all arrested as outlaws. If he didn't want to do that, he could let them struggle on their own. Why risk his reputation to help them?

However, it had to be said that the State of Karensa was successful. The people worked side by side - fisher people, farmers, craftsmen and traders - all prospered.

They lacked one thing only; they did not know or even want to know, either Bellum or the King.

Morwen stood up and brushed sand from her tunic, saying that they should go back to the cave house and unpack the food.

Luke watched her secretly. Her red hair was plaited and coiled around her head to keep her cool and the sleeves of her green tunic were rolled up, revealing freckled arms. She was lovely, inside and out. But she was promised to Esram.

Rolf surprised them all by pulling Morwen back down. His voice was urgent.

"Could you not pledge loyalty to the State? Could you not forget about the King and Salvis and return to your farm? It would be easy to get a pardon if you made the first move."

Morwen smiled a sad, secret smile. "Oh no, Rolf, it would not be easy. It would be the hardest thing in the world for us to do; too hard. You should know that Rolf, if you are our friend."

"Then, my little ones," Rolf's voice was tinged with regret, "may all go well for you. I… have enjoyed your company. These times have been special for me."

He took his leave of them and for a while no-one moved, then Holly, who was never quiet for long, whispered, "He was nearly crying."

"Nearly," Esram said pointedly.

As he spoke, a cold wind arose so they went indoors.

****

From his castle window, Lord Bellum surveyed the island that he believed one day would be his.

The Meadow of Flowers, the Dark Forest, the High Moors leading to the far side of the island; all this he would rule. The State of Karensa would be forgotten. And the King would be forgotten and his son, Salvis, too.

The Guardians, although now useful to Bellum, would also be forgotten. King Bellum would make sure that every person on the island bowed before him to worship.

His desire for worship had been the reason he had disobeyed the King and brought fear to Karensa.

Hawk entered the room and Bellum indicated that he should join him at the window. He gestured to the Meadow of Flowers, far below him.

"My land, Hawk! My people!"

Hawk would be forgotten too!

The young leader of the Guardians bowed. As the ruler of the far side of the island, he was not expected to kneel.

"We have a problem, Hawk," Bellum drawled.

"How is that, my lord? I thought things went well?"

"They do for the most part, but there is one problem and that problem concerns you, or rather, your brother."

"Jay?"

"I believe that is his name."

"I have not seen him since he left home. I heard he was living near the fisher village. The island is now completely under Guardian rule. What could a boy like Jay do to put that at risk?"

Argument angered Bellum. It was disrespectful.

"Your brother, Hawk!" Bellum's voice was as cold and sharp as the black sword he carried at his side. "Your brother now lives in a cave in the Bay of Dolphins with the other outlawed children from that traitor, Petroc's, farm. They think if they lay low and keep quiet they will be left alone. They think no-one knows where they are. But I know! I have those who keep me well informed."

"What about Jay?" Hawk moistened his thin, dry lips.

"Jay has been unwise. He has told some peasant children that ridiculous story about Salvis being alive. They are now telling other children the same story. Jay is a threat and must be removed."

Hawk's knees trembled. He had no great love for Jay but he was still his brother. They shared the same blood.

Bellum, always ready to prey on weakness, knew exactly how to hurt Hawk.

"Hawk, who will you serve? Will it be Jay, your parent's favourite? Or me, who can grant every desire?"

A hundred images flashed across Hawk's mind; memories of being blamed for things Jay had done. Of being thought second best, even though he was cleverer and braver and stronger than Jay would ever be. Of seeing his mother's face light up when Jay entered the room. Of listening to his parent's desire to see their younger son once more and know that he was safe.

Yet it was Hawk who had achieved success, not Jay. Hawk was leader of the Guardians, yet his parents had never once praised him for this achievement.

"Lord Bellum, you know I will always serve you. What must be done?"

Bellum almost purred then he pounced, like a cat.

"I shall tell you exactly what you need to do. You will be rid of your troublesome brother and then you will flourish in your parent's esteem."

Chapter 16

"I know who you are!"

The hot weather continued and a few days later, the young people could not resist a swim in the sea. Soon, they were joined by the dolphins, Telki and Praze.

"We would have to pay loads to swim with dolphins at home," Luke remarked to his sister before splashing over to join Morwen who was floating peacefully, enjoying the quiet moment and dreaming of happier times.

She would rather have been left alone with her thoughts than splash around with Luke, who was a very noisy swimmer.

Rosie and Jay continued to play with the dolphins while Jay and Esram, both strong swimmers, went out into deep water.

"You once told me you could talk to the dolphins in the days before the war," Luke said to Morwen, treading water and making lots of waves.

"I still can," she replied mischievously. "I understand them in a special way."

She was teasing him, but he didn't respond.

"Do you remember what it was like, Morwen, before the war?"

"Oh yes." Her husky voice showed that she was struggling with her own feelings. This was the time she had been thinking about.

"Yes, Luke, how could I forget? We were happy then, Mother and Father and Petroc and me. Then you and Rosie came and learnt to be happy too – except you always wanted to go home. In those days there was no fear or hatred or fighting. I wonder sometimes why the King allowed all this to happen."

"I don't know." Luke considered how much he should share about his own world. "I believe the King knew it would happen and was ready for it. Something like that happened in my world too. It means people can't go to the Great King any more, but the Great King sent his own son to put things right again.

"But that's like our King and Salvis –"

"Just like."

Morwen was thoughtful. "They say Salvis will soon return to Karensa and defeat Bellum then it will be perfect again... I think you and Rosie must go home before that day?"

"Rosie has things to deal with first."

"I know."

"Morwen, if we... if I belonged to Karensa or if you belonged to my world –"

She placed cool fingers over his mouth. "Do not say it. Do not even think about it, Luke. You and me long ago, we were just little children sharing hardship."

"We are not little children now," he said seriously, keeping hold of her hand.

But she snatched it away and swam to the shore. Only when she was safely inside the cave house, did she allow herself to cry.

Later, when they were all dressed, Esram spoke to them seriously as their leader.

"There is hardly any food left and we have not seen Rolf for a few days. We shall have enough for supper but that is all."

"Maybe something has happened to Rolf?" said Holly.

"How could it?" Jay replied. "Rolf governs the entire State of Karensa. What could happen to him? He can do as he pleases."

"There might have been a rebellion." Luke was thinking about news reports on TV at home. That sort of thing often happened in smaller countries.

"Rolf is our only friend," Luke went on. "Without him we should find it hard to survive."

"He spoke in a strange way the last time he was here," Esram pondered. "I still do not like him, but if he doesn't come today we must try to find what has happened. Meanwhile, Luke, my friend, we shall catch fish."

Rolf did not come to them. They ate supper and with only a small amount of bread left for breakfast, Luke and Esram took poles and lines from the back of the cave house and went fishing, using some of their precious bread for bait. They caught a few small fish - enough for one meal, no more.

Long after the others were asleep, Jay lay awake with his thoughts racing. A daring plan was forming in his mind, the thought of which already scared him.

He alone knew the way back across the High Moor to where Holly's father and Esram's uncle were hiding. He could go to them for help.

One thing held him back; fear. He knew he would have to overcome it.

Silently he got up, banging his foot in the dark. He froze, thinking to wake up the other boys, but they were still sleeping soundly. Luke was gently snoring. Muttering under his breath that Salvis would have to help him, Jay crept out of the house, ran across the beach and climbed the cliff steps. His heart was racing and his knees shaking but he forced himself to go on, running swiftly through the coarse grass on the cliff top, going in the direction of the far side of the island.

He never saw the soldiers until it was too late.

The Guardians formed a circle around him, shields held high and swords drawn. He was trapped, like a wild animal.

Strong hands held his arms and he looked up into his brother's eyes.

For a brief moment his hopes were raised, but one look at Hawk's face told him he could expect no mercy. Like Petroc before him, Jay was going to die.

But Jay was not as focused as Petroc, or as stubborn, or as brave. Unlike Petroc, Jay had no home to fight for. All he had was his loyalty to the King and he was afraid, so afraid, this would not be enough to keep him strong.

Luke was the first to notice that Jay was missing. Leaving Esram sleeping, Luke went down to the beach to look for his friend. He might have gone fishing, for he had wanted to come with them last night and said he would have caught plenty of fish but Esram had insisted he stay to protect the girls. He had not been pleased.

When there was no sign of Jay on the beach, Luke began to feel uneasy and hurried back to wake the others.

"He will have gone for a walk," said Holly, rubbing sleep from her eyes. "Jay does that sort of thing. I have known him for years. He likes to think about stuff."

Luke disagreed. "Something's happened. I know it."

Rosie supported him. "Jay wouldn't just have walked away. It's much too dangerous. Jay is too… too sensible to do anything like that."

Morwen was trembling.

"There is danger!" she exclaimed. "Jay is in great danger. I feel it in my heart."

"You are right," said a familiar voice from the doorway. Rolf's shadow was blocking out the light.

Rosie squealed. She was hungry. "Rolf! I knew you would come! Have you brought some food?"

"Brought you food?" The ruler's voice was strangely cold. "Why would I bring food to the enemies of the State? Guards, arrest them all!"

They were too shocked to even cry out in surprise. Suddenly, the cave house was full of armed soldiers, all wearing the hated Guardian uniform and now, once again bearing the emblem of the silver serpent on their tunics and shields.

"I discovered your hiding place," Rolf lied. "Now, you must be taken to the village to stand trial."

"What?" Luke shouted. "Why?"

He knew the answer and he was right.

"Treason," Rolf replied blandly. "You are all enemies of Karensa and you will all be tried for treason."

Perhaps Salvis gave him the courage, perhaps it was because Morwen looked so scared, but somehow Luke found hidden strength.

"Rolf," he said with a boldness he did not feel, "I will make you an offer. The Guardians are more interested in me than the others. Bellum and me, we are old enemies. If I come willingly with you, then you can take me to Bellum's castle and he will be pleased with you. Only let the others go free to serve their King."

Rolf laughed. He threw back his head and roared with laughter, deep, musical laughter that was somehow familiar to them.

"Do I need to bargain with you like a market trader? Why should I do that when I already have you all?"

When in great danger, people react in different ways. Holly became angry. It was clear that Rolf had deceived them and betrayed them. Holly hated liars and she never gave in without a fight.

She kicked Rolf's shin. She kicked very hard and Rolf cried out in pain and anger.

Horrified, the young people watched as his pale eyes glinted with strange, amber lights.

Now they knew why he had reminded them of someone since the day they first met him.

"It's Bellum!" Luke muttered. "You must be one of Bellum's men!"

Rolf took hold of Luke by his hair and jerked his head backwards. Luke clenched his teeth and did not cry out.

"Oh, I am much more than Bellum's man, Luke. Can you not see who I really am, you of all people, who have crossed Bellum so many times? Oh Luke, you know me, don't you?"

"I know who you are," Rosie said quietly and calmly. "You are more than one of Bellum's men. You have his looks and his voice and his eyes. You have to be his son!"

Chapter 17

To Trust the King

Jay had never thought he would go back home as a prisoner. He had never thought he would stand trial as a traitor. He had never thought that telling two children about the King would be a crime on the island of Karensa. He had never thought that his judge would be his own brother.

The trial was soon over and he was found guilty. Two scared little children had been called as witnesses. When asked if Jay had forced them to listen to him, they nodded silently and that was proof enough for Hawk.

Jay stood in chains in the judgement hall of the Guardians House, a small, frightened figure trying bravely to trust the King.

Hawk spoke sternly. "I am sorry that it has come to this Jay; that I must sit in judgement on my own brother."

Jay knew that if he tried to speak his teeth would chatter. He did not want Hawk to know he was terrified.

Hawk took his silence for insolence. "Jay, you have been found guilty of treason. Can you think of nothing to say in your defence that I might spare you? I do not recall you being so quiet in the past!"

Jay hung his head and said nothing.

"When we were younger you could not wait to tell tales to Father or Mother," Hawk insisted. He sneered contemptuously. "Try going to them now! They cannot help you any more!"

All at once Jay realised that this was not about the King or Salvis or the Guardians; this was about two brothers, one who was favoured by their parents and the other one who was criticized.

The terror that had held Jay's tongue disappeared. He knew he faced death because age was not a consideration in Guardian law. Yet Hawk's display of jealousy helped him through his fear.

"Your law found me guilty, not the King's law." Now his voice was as steady as a rock. "The King's judgement would be that Lord Bellum is the traitor."

"Ah, but the King has no power here!"

"Oh yes he does have power! You will one day learn of his power, Hawk."

"So is that your defence? Don't you have anything to say to save yourself? No excuses? I recall you were always good at making excuses, especially if they showed me in a bad light."

Jay was incredibly calm and bold. "If I did that, then I was wrong and I am sorry," he said, choosing his words with care. "Hawk, we are brothers. We share the same blood. When I was little I wanted to be like you but you never seemed to have any time for me. You never wanted me around. No matter what you do, you will always be my brother. I love you because you are my brother."

Hawk stared at him. This was the very last thing he expected to hear. He looked Jay in the eye and knew that he was telling the truth, and not simply seeking mercy.

"What is more," Jay added suddenly, and for no apparent reason, "the King loves you even more than I do. Even though you hate him, the King still loves you."

Hawk opened his mouth to speak and then closed it again. There seemed to be a power surrounding Jay that Hawk did not understand, but it was something he wanted for himself.

Hawk gave in. He wanted to help Jay and he wanted to receive the King's power and the Guardians did not seem important any more.

How could the King forgive him, though? He had fought against him and imprisoned his followers.

Long ago, Jay and some other children had taken this same message to their parents and they had become followers of the King. Hawk had refused to listen. Maybe, secretly, his parents still followed the King's ways?

"Ask your King to forgive me!" he whispered in a strange voice that did not sound like his own.

"I can't do that. You must ask him yourself," said Jay. "Make Salvis you lord now, Hawk, so I shall know you belong to the King before... before..."

"You are not going to die," Hawk assured him. Then Jay helped him as he promised to serve the King and Salvis forever.

When it was done, for the first time in his life, Hawk knew true happiness. He threw his arms around his young brother then shouted to the soldiers to remove Jay's chains and then he sent them away.

"They are not pleased," said Hawk as soon as they were on their own. "It will not be long before Lord Bellum finds out what I have done. You must leave now. You must return to the other side of the island, to the Fisher Village and farms."

There was even more danger there, but Jay had no choice.

So he ran. It was one thing Jay was good at. He ran from the Guardian's House and away from the town. He ran towards the High Moor, but he was not going to the Bay of Dolphins. He made up his mind to find Holly's father and Esram's uncle on the High Moor. His legs took him faster and faster to the one place he was sure he would be safe.

However, that was not to be for once again, Veritan intervened. The great Lord of the Palace waited for him on the lower slopes of the moor. Without a word he lifted Jay onto his grey horse and together they rode faster than the west wind across the moor in the direction of the Dark Forest.

There, Lord Veritan told him to wait in a special place he knew of, a hidden cave of ferns, deep within the forest.

Jay was hungry and thirsty and once again the fear returned to haunt him but he pushed it aside.

His adventure had given him a confidence he did not have before and he liked it. He was an ordinary boy, not clever or rich or powerful. Yet in the face of death he had been brave. All he had needed to do was to trust the King.

The young people huddled together in the cave house. If Rolf really was Bellum's son, they could expect no mercy. It was over. The battle was lost. All they could do now was to trust in the King and look forward to being with Salvis in the Royal Palace.

'I shall see my friends again,' Rosie thought. It helped.

Morwen stepped forward. She did not question the Guardian's right to arrest them as Luke or Holly might do; that was not her way.

Instead she asked humbly that they might have a few moments together before the guards took them away.

"For the sake of happy times we shared, Rolf," she added, her eyes downcast.

Luke had never admired her as much as he did now.

Rolf agreed. Morwen was lovely, inside and out, and few people would deny such a request.

"Maiden, for the sake of those times I will give you five minutes alone." He turned to his men who were muttering amongst themselves. "How can they escape? There is only one door and we shall stand outside that… The children shall have five minutes before we leave."

He led the mutinous Guardians outside to wait on the cliff steps. When the young people were alone there seemed to be nothing they wanted to say so they simply held on to one another for what could be the last time.

While they were standing like this, Esram reached out to take Morwen in his arms. As he moved he lost his balance and fell against the wooden wall at the back of the cave house. With a loud crash, the wall gave way and Esram fell through to the other side.

He staggered to his feet, coughing and spluttering. "Quick," he whispered urgently, "someone get a light!"

Luke passed him the oil lamp which in the dark cave was always kept burning. In its flickering light a tunnel was revealed; a long, downhill tunnel supported by wooden beams.

"It's the entrance to a mine shaft!" Luke gasped excitedly. "We have them just like this at home in Cornwall. Come on, it's our only chance!"

He did not add that these mine shafts were dangerous. This was their only escape. One by one they piled through the gap in the wall into damp and darkness.

Esram, who was the tallest, held the lamp as high as he could to give everyone light as they stumbled along the dark tunnel.

Behind them, they heard the soldiers shout angrily when they realised their prisoners had escaped.

With the shouting came another, more sinister sound, a low rumbling which quickly grew louder.

"It's a rock fall behind us!" Luke cried.

Rosie cheered. "It will cut them off and that means they can't follow us. We are safe!"

"No we're not," Luke said slowly as realisation dawned. "You never think things through, Rosie. The Guardians can't follow us, but we can't go back either. We're trapped in here."

It was later that day when Rolf visited his father's castle. Lord Bellum sat in his throne-like chair under the canopy of black velvet and he laughed aloud as Rolf told him of the children's fate.

"You have done well, my son! I hoped that the children would join me. The girl, Rosie, is a gifted singer and I would have given her a high place in my kingdom, but she would take nothing I offered. It is their choice. If they oppose me, I am happy for them to die in this way."

"They cannot get out of the mine shaft, Father. They will be sealed up. These children will trouble you no more and for that I am well pleased. It's just that... the eldest girl, Morwen... "

"Ah, Morwen is special... But she had her chance too and like the others, she refused."

"One thing, Father... Some say that Salvis is on the move. What of him?"

"What of Salvis?" Bellum's voice was scornful. "I myself killed Salvis. He cannot return. People look to you, now, Rolf. You are their deliverer. You have united the island of Karensa and brought peace and this has encouraged the people to turn away from the King. Now I will be able to take control and the King and his Palace will be gone for ever."

Chapter 18

Special Friends

There was no way back so they were forced to carry on. The tunnel took them ever downwards, deeper and deeper below the island. Its walls were supported by thick, wooden beams. Scuttling feet suggested rats but Luke told his sister they were mice. Rats scared her.

Esram went in front with the flickering lamp. The oil was burning low. Holly wished she had filled it when Morwen had asked her. She and Rosie kept close to the light. Then came Morwen and last of all Luke, whose task was to make sure no-one was left behind or hurt.

Holly was every bit as scared as Rosie, but that did not stop her from wondering about Jay.

"Where did he go? What if the Guardians took him?"

Rosie squeezed her hand. "Jay's brother is leader of the Guardians. He won't hurt Jay. We shall find him. He's probably wondering where we are, right this minute."

"You are funny, Rosie," replied Holly and Rosie never did know what she meant.

As they crept along, the tunnel became wet and very slippery.

"If there is water there must be a way out," Luke reasoned unconvincingly.

Esram stopped so abruptly that Holly and Rosie bumped into him.

"I cannot believe this is real!" he muttered.

He shone the lamp to his right and its dim light revealed that their path was hardly more than a ledge overlooking a water-filled cavern. The cavern, like the tunnel was supported by wooden beams.

"The mine must have flooded years ago," said Luke who was familiar with disused mine shafts back in Cornwall and knew about such things.

No-one was ever sure what happened next. Morwen gave a cry of alarm. Then she disappeared.

"She's gone into the water!" Esram cried.

Luke disagreed. "She didn't, there was no splash." He took the lamp from Esram and knelt down, shining the light over the edge of the path.

Morwen lay on a second ledge beneath them. Her eyes were closed. Blood trickled down her face.

Luke didn't stop to think. Morwen needed him. With a single movement he slipped over the ledge and dropped down to where she lay. The landing jarred his legs but he hardly noticed the pain.

He lifted Morwen in his strong arms, grateful for the many hours he had spent in training for the school Rugby team.

Her eyelids fluttered and she moaned softly.

"She's alive!" he shouted.

"We must get you up!" Esram cried, always the practical one. He lay on his stomach while the two girls held his legs. "If I hold out my hands I can just about reach you... Morwen, can you stand?"

She was dazed. Blood oozed from her forehead. Luke's hands were gentle as he helped her to stand up.

"Reach up!" Esram ordered. As she swayed dizzily, his voice took on a new authority. "Morwen do as I tell you. Reach up towards me now!"

Morwen's face was deathly white and Luke thought that Esram was too harsh. He would never have spoken to her in that way.

Then he realised that Esram knew Morwen better than he did because she responded by obediently raising her arms.

Luke lifted her off the ground and Esram reached down as far as he could while the girls clung tightly to his legs so that he didn't fall over the edge and Morwen was hauled to safety.

"Now you, Luke," Esram commanded in the same harsh tones that held no room for argument.

Luke tried to reach Esram's outstretched hands but his arms were not quite long enough and he had no-one to lift him.

"You'll have to jump!" Esram told him. "Jump up and I'll catch you!"

Luke looked up to him and then at the narrow ledge and then down to the lake far below. If his foot slipped, if he fell in that water there would be no way he could ever get out again.

Taking a deep breath he yelled, "I'm coming now! Be ready!"

He leapt as high as he could. Esram groaned with pain as their hands made contact and Esram was suddenly forced to take a weight greater than his own.

His back jarred excruciatingly. His arms felt as though they had been pulled out of their sockets.

But with Rosie and Holly supporting him, he held on. Luke was pulled to safety and was soon being hugged by his sister.

Almost as soon as his feet touched safe ground, the oil lamp expired and they were plunged into total darkness.

Only, it wasn't total darkness. They could still see each other. Luke could still see Rosie even when she moved away from him.

"Look!" Rosie shouted triumphantly. "The tunnel is going upwards again. I can see daylight. There must be another way out!"

Esram forgot about Morwen for a moment and laughed with relief. "We're saved!"

"Not quite," said Luke, looking down at the deep, dark water. "We've still got to get out of here and this path is wicked narrow."

Esram did not understand how a path could be wicked. He had never heard Luke say that before.

Holly shuddered. "Let's get out of here, quick as we can!"

"Hold fast." Suddenly Esram was being serious. "Luke, before we go on, you risked your own life to save Morwen. Thank you does not seem enough."

"It will do," Luke replied gruffly. "It's not needed, anyway. Morwen is… Morwen…"

"No, Holly is right. We should get out of here as soon as we can," Rosie said firmly. "If we have to thank anybody except Luke, maybe it should be the King? He has been with us and helped us all through everything. I believe the King showed us the way out of here. We have to trust the King."

There was nothing they could say to that so, with Esram helping Morwen, they pressed onwards and upwards until at last they found a cleft in the rock.

With a yell of victory, Luke squeezed through it, pushing aside a clump of thick fern.

The others followed, rubbing their eyes against the sudden daylight.

Jay was waiting for them there.

Stories were exchanged of their separate adventures and afterwards they were strangely excited and subdued, happy and weary all at the same time.

Luke regarded his surroundings as though seeing them for the first time. They were in the Dark Forest, in a small woodland cave made from ferns and overhanging bushes.

"I... we... I've been here before," he faltered. "This is the place we met up with Holly and Esram, the last time me and Rosie came here. It's the place I got my scar, that night in the blizzard. Look, there's the sharp branch I fell on."

His hand touched the white scar he carried on his shoulder.

"Petroc was with us then," said Rosie sadly.

Luke, quite out of character, cried, "I wish he was here now! Oh, I do wish he was here now!"

""Oh so do I," whispered Morwen. "Oh, how I would love to see my brother again."

Rosie felt as though a sharp knife had pierced her heart. What was it about Karensa that made your feelings so strong?

Holly swallowed back her tears. She had not known Petroc very well, but she had liked him.

"Is Hawk really one of us now?" Holly asked curiously. "And Jay, I cannot believe you were so brave."

Jay's pale face turned dark crimson. "You don't know how scared I was," he admitted. "You don't have to be brave, Holly. You need to trust the King. He does the rest."

"Rosie, what are you doing?" Luke's sister was on her hands and knees, scrabbling in the undergrowth.

"Got it!" she said triumphantly. Opening her hand she showed him a small piece of stiff cardboard.

"It's the missing jigsaw piece." Luke whispered. "How did you find that?"

Rosie felt tears prick her eyes. She did not know why. "You know what this means, don't you? We are going home."

Holly and Morwen began to cry at exactly the same time. Jay gave Holly a hug. It didn't help at all.

Morwen whispered to Luke. "Walk with me a little way into the forest?"

Esram nodded his agreement, and Morwen took Luke's hand and guided him further into the Dark Forest.

When they were quite alone, she turned to face him and took his big hands in her own small ones. Her green eyes were sad. Her face was streaked with blood and tears.

She sighed deeply. "I would love to ask you to stay but I know you cannot. I feel that this time when you go home, you will never again return."

Luke was willing this not to be happening but he knew that what she said was true.

"Morwen, the first time me and Rosie came to Karensa, you and I were close friends. You said that we were just children sharing hardship. Do you still say that?"

"No… no it was not so. I did not tell the truth that day. You were always special to me, Luke, even when we were little children. You know that. Maybe it was just the dangers that we faced together, but that does not mean our feelings were any less real"

"If things were different –"

"Ssh! Luke, things are not different. We were never meant to be together. I have Esram, who loves me and I love him too, in a different way that will last and help us to build a family when we are older and get married. Even if you stayed on Karensa, I would still marry Esram for he is my chosen one and I am his. He made me happy when I thought I would never smile again."

"Then why-"

"Why am I saying all this? Because it needs to be said, because we shall never have another chance to talk, because we are very special friends. You are much more than a brother to me."

Her own tears prevented her from saying more. They never knew how long they stood together, knowing that when they parted, they would never meet again.

Luke was no longer a child, nor yet a man, but he was old enough to know that some things were simply not meant to be.

For the first and last time ever, he kissed her. Then he let her go.

Rosie was waiting for them. She was crying too.

"She hugged Morwen. "You are like a sister to me. Say goodbye for us!" she gasped, then without another word, Luke and Rosie ran off together, deep into the Dark Forest, trusting the King to show them the way.

Chapter 19

The Day of the White Horse

Luke and Rosie paused at the place where the Dark Forest met a grassy meadow, always a special place for those who still followed the King, yet a place that his enemies could not find.

Across the meadow, they gazed upon the brilliance and splendour of the Royal Palace.

Not far beyond this beautiful palace stood the dark, brooding outline of Bellum's castle, but compared with the Royal Palace, this castle was insignificant.

"We won't ever come here again, will we?" said Luke. It was a question that did not need an answer.

He had been very quiet since they said goodbye to Morwen. Rosie was wise not to ask questions and even wiser not to try to comfort him.

She opened her hand and looked at the piece of jigsaw. A quiet whisper in her heart had told her where it was hidden, but that was her secret. The picture on it could be part of an animal but they would not really know until it was fitted into the puzzle.

"No, I don't think we ever will return," she agreed. "Let's remember as much as we can of everything before we go home."

They closed their eyes and tried to paint a picture on their memories; a picture of the Royal Palace; the golden turrets and silver pennants, the light which shone from the stone walls.

They could not paint the feeling that surrounded and flowed from the King's Palace but they could feel it and save it, deep in their hearts.

Luke looked up first. "Something's happening at the Royal Palace, Rosie! Look!"

They gazed in wonder as the Palace doors swung open. At the very same moment, Bellum's castle shuddered as though hit by a mighty earthquake. The air was filled with beautiful music unlike any song that human voices could sing; words older than time and sweeter than tomorrow's dawn, secret words of ancient days, words of great power and beauty.

Time stood still as this wonderful sound was lifted by the breeze and carried to the furthest ends of the island.

A rider stood at the gate of the Palace; a man who was more than a man, and the horse he rode was white. This magnificent beast grew impatient, pawing the ground and tossing his silver mane and tail. He was anxious to complete the task for which he had been created.

"It's Salvis! He's coming back," Luke said breathlessly. It was difficult to speak, so awesome was the sight before them and so wonderful the music.

It was indeed Lord Salvis, son of the King, but it was not the Salvis they remembered for now he was revealed in his true glory.

His amazing love now burned like fire from his dark eyes. He was dressed in a white tunic and trousers, slashed with crimson. Around his head was a crown of flashing light which was never still so that he was surrounded by a moving aura. Golden light shone from his face, the brilliance of which hurt their eyes.

"Mighty Lord!" cried Rosie, and without any prompting they fell to the ground and covered their eyes.

They did not see the Rider draw his sword but the light from its blade travelled the distance between them as though it was no distance at all. It touched them, searching, forgiving, healing…

118

Rosie sobbed as her grief for lost friends faded away as though lifted by a mighty hand. All sorrow was gone. All that remained were wonderful memories.

In place of sadness, Salvis gave her peace and understanding. The King's son had healed her.

Luke's own failings were brought to light by his searching presence and once again he asked to be forgiven.

Never was there such love, such mercy, yet there was also sadness for the things that might have been.

They knew they could not stay to witness Salvis' defeat of Bellum. That was for the people of Karensa. Luke and Rosie belonged to their own world.

Holding tightly to each other with Rosie still clutching the lost jigsaw piece, they prepared to go home.

As the White Horse stepped forward, every creature on Karensa praised the King in the manner of its creation. Birds in the Dark Forest added their song to the music of the Royal Palace. Dolphins leapt higher than ever above the waves to celebrate the return of their lord.

Hearts were lifted and filled with joy and the hope of a bright, wonderful future when Salvis reigned in peace.

This was the memory Luke and Rosie took home; that love had defeated evil and the final victory would go to the King.

When they looked up again, the soft, green grass of the meadows of Karensa had been replaced by the scratchy dining room carpet and they were in their cottage at Poldawn.

They scrambled to their feet. The bookshelves were as they had always remembered them and the hidden door was no longer there. The jigsaw was where they had left it on the dining room table.

They were stunned into silence by what they had seen. They were sad to leave their friends behind yet relieved to be in the safety of their own home.

Without words, Rosie fitted the last piece into the puzzle. They were not really surprised that the figure at the Palace gate was a Rider on a White Horse.

"Look Rosie, look behind the white horse," Luke muttered. "There is someone with red hair."

"Oh it's Petroc," said Rosie, and her healing was complete.

They were silent for a while but it was a happy silence. No words could ever describe how they were feeling.

"Salvis didn't look like Salvis any more, and the horse looked bigger than when we saw him in the Dark Forest," said Rosie at last.

Luke thought he understood. "Salvis needs to be more than an ordinary man for this work. He has to defeat Bellum and win the people back for the King."

When he had finished speaking, a hush descended on the room and just as it had done in the meadow, a wonderful feeling flowed into their hearts. It was every bit as strong as it had been on the island. Then, just as suddenly, it was gone.

"Salvis was here," whispered Rosie. "Salvis was here yet he can't really have been here 'cos he lives on Karensa."

"It wasn't Salvis," Luke whispered back. "It can't be Salvis, can it? You know who it really was, don't you?"

"Yes," she agreed. "We both know."

"We both know," he echoed, but although he should be happy, he sounded sad.

"Poor Luke, Salvis has taken away my sadness but you still have yours. Will you miss Morwen so much?"

Luke smiled wryly. "It will only be for a little while. Well, I shall miss her of course but I suppose I've always known we were not meant to be together. She lives on Karensa and we live here and she has Esram to look after her now."

It was then that Luke knew he had grown up and what was more, Rosie knew he had grown up too.

"You do love her though?" she prompted. After all, she was his sister and it was her duty to find out about these things. She wasn't really being nosy.

"Yes I do," he replied and the sound of their parent's car outside gave him the perfect excuse he needed not to say any more.

Chapter 20

Faithful and True

When Dad and Stacey returned, Luke and Rosie were sitting one at either end of the sofa. Because time was different on Karensa, the young people had not been missed, even though they had spent many months on the island.

"You two look a little guilty," said Dad. "What have you done?"

"Nothing wrong!" they chorused.

Stacey sat between them. She was flushed and happy. Dad hovered over them like a teacher, Rosie thought.

"We've got something to tell you," said Dad, trying not to sound excited but failing.

"We're not sure how you will feel about this," added Stacey, "but – oh, there's no easy way to say this. We've just come from the hospital and we have some special news for you."

"You're not ill?" Luke exclaimed. Their real mother had been ill and had died when they were very young.

Dad quickly reassured them. "No - far from it - Luke, Rosie, you're going to have a baby brother."

The news was met with silence. Then Rosie beamed.

"You're having a baby, Stacey?"

"Yes, Rosie," Stacey laughed. "Your Dad and I are going to have a baby of our own!"

Just then their dog, Pepper, came in to tell them that it was time for her to be fed. Luke called to the little collie and hid his face in her soft fur. He was not sure how he felt about this news. A new baby could mean that he and

Rosie were pushed to one side. Even as the thought entered his mind another one replaced it.

Don't worry.

"How do you know it's a boy?" he said warily. "It might be a girl."

"No." Stacey shook her head. "I've been to the hospital today and they are certain that the baby is a boy. Look, here is the scan photo. Meet your brother."

They studied the strange photograph. They could see a head and arms and legs. Rosie said it was cool.

But Luke already had a brother. He and Petroc had long ago sworn brotherhood.

Rosie imagined how he must feel and had an idea. "Could we... I mean could Luke and me pick a name for the baby?"

Stacey smiled. She had not known what to expect when they told her step children the news. Picking a name was a small thing to ask.

"I don't see why not," she replied. "What do you want to call him?"

"Petroc," they replied firmly and at the same time.

"You both sound very sure. Well, Petroc's a good name. I like it," Stacey agreed.

Dad noticed the jigsaw on the dining room table and went to have a look.

"I didn't know you two liked jigsaws. Did you buy this one from the church sale? Wait a moment this place looks somehow familiar... Luke, come over here."

Dad placed his hand on Luke's shoulder as they stood side by side surveying the circular puzzle.

"This place... there was an island that your mum used to talk about, a place with dolphins, remember? Or were you too young?"

Luke's mouth felt dry. "I remember."

"She wrote a song about it, something about dolphins and rainbows."

"*Where dolphins race with Rainbows,*" Rosie said in a hushed voice.

"That's right! She claimed she had once been there. Now that must be the place she called High Hill, and those are the woods called the Dark Forest. The building in the centre has to be the Royal Palace. She never mentioned the other castle though, or that farm. This must be the Bay of Dolphins. She talked a lot about this island, especially when she was ill. She said it was a special place that not many people find. It had a name, Karibeth, or Kinsa or something."

"Karensa," Luke murmured. "It's called Karensa and Dad, we've been there too."

In the same way they used to stand at the farm gate on the island, Luke and Rosie now stood at the gate at the end of their own garden. This gate led to a creek where the rowing boat that had first taken them to Karensa was moored.

"My mother wrote songs," Rosie breathed. "Like me, I write songs. She wrote the *Dolphins* song. You used to sing that, Luke, and they knew it on Karensa too. My mother could have taught it to them."

They were awed to learn that their mother had been to the island before them. She would have walked through the cool trees of the Dark Forest and climbed High Hill and splashed in the sea at the Bay of Dolphins, just as they had done.

"It all fits," Luke said. "The first time we went to the island I dreamed that Mum was telling me to find the place where dolphins raced with rainbows. I dreamed it again when we were in prison and thought we might die.

Of course, she must have been there herself or how would she know about it?"

"Jay and Holly said there had been other visitors before us," said Rosie. "Everything makes sense now."

Luke got serious then and started to talk about the Bible. He did that sometimes. Rosie was used to it. She was cool about it. When he grew older he wanted to do missionary work.

"The Bible says that God works all things to the good for those who follow him."

"That's what he's done with us then. I shall always be sad that Petroc died but it doesn't hurt like it used to. Now we've come home, where we belong to be."

As she spoke those words, a wintry sun came out. Unusually for this time of year, a huge rainbow appeared over the sea, the brightest rainbow they had ever seen, so bright that a second rainbow was reflected beneath it. Between the two rainbows they saw Karensa, a jewel beyond price, shimmering and sparkling in the sunlight.

Luke touched his shoulder again. His scar had vanished. He showed Rosie the place where it had been.

"It means we really can't go back," she said sadly.

"We won't need to any more. We need to get on with out lives now."

"Luke... d'you remember when Morwen and Esram did that betrothed thing? Morwen took her flowers to his grave beneath the cherry tree and said that Petroc was the best brother in the world."

Luke nodded. How could he forget that sad moment?

"Well, I know we fall out sometimes, but... Luke, I think you're the best brother in the world."

Luke dare not reply. He might cry and crying was ok for Karensa but it wasn't ok here.

The rainbows faded and Karensa faded with them. They knew that when they returned to the house the jigsaw would have disappeared.

Their adventures on the island were over but the great adventure of lives spent following Jesus was only just beginning.

Salvis guided the White Horse, slowly and deliberately from the Royal Palace.

The horse walked proudly. This was his destiny. For such a time as this, he was born.

Following Salvis there rode a vast company of Palace servants, all clothed in pure white.

Leading the servants was a young man with green eyes and bright red hair; Petroc was following the Lord to whom and for whom he had surrendered his life.

A mighty call to battle resounded from the Royal Palace and at the sound of its golden notes, the walls of Bellum's dark castle crumbled.

With a shout of triumph, prisoners were set free. Bellum's followers wailed with fear as their stronghold fell for they knew that the day of their final judgement had arrived.

Slowly, very slowly and with great purpose, the mighty army rode towards the crumbling stronghold, there to do battle once and forever with the powers of darkness.

Lord Veritan raised his golden sword and Petroc lifted high a white, silken banner and the procession moved away from the Royal Palace, out into the island. The King watched from the Royal Palace, unseen but mighty in power.

As they moved forward, every drop of blood that had ever been shed for the King rose up from the ground as a priceless ruby; every tear that had fallen became a shining pearl; every battle bravely fought was a sparkling diamond.

These treasures were cast before the white horse and made a path that glistened with precious jewels of sacrifice.

It was along this path that Salvis, always Faithful and True, rode to victory.

Creatures of the Dark Forest lifted their heads to receive this moment for which they had waited so long; this time when once again they would live in peace with humankind.

Dolphins, leaping through the waves, cast wonderful rainbows behind them, rejoicing that the old was over and the new had come.

With a mighty trumpet call, the mist surrounding Karensa was lifted and all things were made perfect as Lord Salvis rode out to take back the Lost Kingdom

Then I saw heaven open, and there was a white horse. Its rider is called Faithful and true; it is with justice that he judges and fights his battles.

Revelation 16 verse 11

Lightning Source UK Ltd.
Milton Keynes UK
26 August 2010

159013UK00001B/3/P